"What Are You Doing Here?"

As he spoke, his hands tightened on the pizza box. What he wanted was to touch her face, and he was annoyed at the strength of his reaction.

"I was afraid I'd miss you and you'd start working without me." She put the bouquet on top of the box. "I don't welsh on my promises."

"Nice to know." He nodded at the flowers. "Who gave *these* to you?"

"Nobody. I bought them for you."

Her answer left him speechless for a moment. This was a first, he thought. *She* was a first, for a lot of things. It had him worried. He cleared his throat. "No luck with the auditions?"

"There aren't any until the end of the week. I'm all yours until then."

Oh, how he wished it were true!

Dear Reader,

Welcome to Silhouette! Our goal is to give you hours of unbeatable reading pleasure, and we hope you'll enjoy each month's six new Silhouette Desires. These sensual, provocative love stories are both believable and compelling—sometimes they're poignant, sometimes humorous, but always enjoyable.

Indulge yourself. Experience all the passion and excitement of falling in love along with our heroine as she meets the irresistible man of her dreams and together they overcome all obstacles in the path to a happy ending.

If this is your first Desire, I hope it'll be the first of many. If you're already a Silhouette Desire reader, thanks for your support! Look for some of your favorite authors in the coming months: Stephanie James, Diana Palmer, Dixie Browning, Ann Major and Doreen Owens Malek, to name just a few.

Happy reading!

Isabel Swift
Senior Editor

SDRL-7/85

MARIE NICOLE
Chocolate Dreams

Silhouette Desire
Published by Silhouette Books New York

America's Publisher of Contemporary Romance

SILHOUETTE BOOKS
300 East 42nd St., New York, N.Y. 10017

Copyright © 1987 by Marie Rydzynski-Ferrarella

ISBN: 0-373-05346-0

First Silhouette Books printing April 1987

America's Publisher of Contemporary Romance

Printed in the U.S.A.

MARIE NICOLE

is a natural romance writer because her own life has been so romantic. She met her husband-to-be in tenth grade and began dating him in college. The first time he kissed her he made the room fade away, and things have only gotten better for them since.

To Michael,
who must be ninety-seven
percent chocolate by now.
With love, Marysia.

One

Teddi had never been particularly afraid of the dark. As a child, dimly lit, shadow-filled places had ceased to hold unknown terrors after she had learned that ghosts, goblins and things that went bump in the night didn't really exist except in overfertile imaginations.

Except for now.

She felt an unaccustomed queasiness forming in the pit of her stomach. With a conscious effort she stepped up her pace. She hadn't thought this section of Manhattan would be quite so seedy. She looked neither left nor right.

You're acting like a typical out-of-towner, she told herself. Stories about the dangers of New York City are exaggerated. But it was like whistling in the dark.

There were lots of people on the street. Anywhere else that would have made her feel safe, but here they were the reason for her uneasiness. Bathed in the bright light flashing from marquees overhead, the people in the area were a conglomeration of the lurid and the poor. Some moved quickly, some not at all. Some whispered; others shouted. They all appeared somehow unfriendly and threatening. For the first time in her life Teddi had the sensation of being totally isolated. The word "mugged" found its way into her consciousness.

She realized now that it had been a stupid decision to walk from the Port Authority at this time of night, but, then, how could she have known that it was located in such a run-down area? Allowing only her eyes to move, she scanned Eighth Avenue for a taxi. There had been a whole fleet of them when she had walked out of the bus terminal. Now there wasn't a single one in sight.

She switched her canvas suitcase from her left hand to her right. The handle was beginning to pinch the skin on her palm. When she had left the bus and walked through the Port Authority terminal the area had seemed so populated with travelers that she had decided to take in a little of the city and walk to the Y. At the time it had seemed like a good idea. At the time.

She pressed her lips together and kept walking.

Teddi thought she heard footsteps directly behind her.

Of course there are footsteps behind you, she told herself. There were hundreds of people around, even though it was getting late. Back home, ten o'clock meant that the sidewalks were all but rolled up. Here it didn't seem to matter what time it was. But that was why she had come, wasn't it? To sample life at its fullest. There wasn't all that much to sample in Willow Grove, and she knew there had to be more challenges to be met than just making it through the day. She wanted to grab life with both hands and hold on for the ride.

She couldn't shake the feeling that someone was following her.

Don't let your imagination run away with you, she warned herself, refusing to look over her shoulder. Alice always said you had an overactive imagination. She thought of her eldest sister, so sedate, so set in her ways. They all were. All four of her sisters. They had looked at her as if she were crazy when she had announced her plans to go to New York to be a dancer on Broadway. But, then, they were happy with their small-town existence. It suited them, just the way it had their mother. But Teddi had always felt restless, as if she didn't belong, as if she were waiting for something. Something more. When she turned twenty-one she had decided that she wasn't going to wait any longer. She was going to go out and meet her destiny.

She wondered if Destiny was walking behind her right now.

"Hey, pretty lady, why are you running away from me?"

The words sent a cold shiver down her spine despite the almost suffocating heat of the July night. Her fear metamorphosed into anger at the man for making her feel this way. She wanted to swing around and answer him tartly. But since discretion really was the better part of valor, she knew that it would be wiser just to keep walking.

Where was that damn building? she thought impatiently. A friend of her mother's who had been to New York several years ago had advised Teddi that the best place for her to stay would be at the YWCA on Eighth Avenue and Fiftieth Street. Teddi had planned to spend the night there and begin the chore of finding an apartment early the next morning.

How are you going to find an apartment when you can't even find a hotel? she asked herself irritably.

Teddi had already passed Fiftieth Street. Maybe she had gotten the street wrong. She'd already walked by several hotels, but they were all run-down and looked like the types that charged by the hour instead of the night.

"That's what I like. Playing hard to get. But honey, I don't like to get all sweaty, and it's hot out tonight."

Teddi took a deep breath. Just walk, she ordered herself. Don't think. There's bound to be a policeman around somewhere.

Instead of a comforting blue uniform, she saw women languishing in the doorways, peering out at her, their faces hard, their eyes as cold and lifeless as the poses they struck. They were waiting for takers.

Why didn't the man who was following her stop to pay attention to one of them?

The backs of her legs began to ache. The canvas suitcase banged against her shin. She noted the pain dully.

Maybe if I head toward Fifth Avenue, she told herself, I'll feel better. A definite uneasiness was beginning to set in. She had studied a map of New York on the bus and knew that she had to turn right while walking uptown to get to Fifth Avenue. Maybe the character behind her would be frightened off by the better section of town, the way a vampire was frightened away by daylight.

She certainly hoped so.

She crossed at the corner and made her way down the long, dark street.

Store windows, dark and devoid of life at this late hour, were lined up like a mournful Greek chorus on both sides of the street. She saw a derelict huddled on a stoop, a brown paper bag clutched in his hand even in sleep. Her heart rate quickened.

If that bus hadn't broken down, she would have arrived here at six. There was still plenty of daylight at six o'clock in July. There would have been plenty of time to get settled, even if she had misplaced the Y. Her anxiety grew.

Keith yawned as he brought his cab to a stop at the light, then chuckled. He was getting old, he thought. Yawning at ten o'clock. It hadn't been so long ago that he could stay up round the clock. But those were the days when he didn't have a dream haunting him. A dream, his father had shouted, that belonged to an idiot.

"What kind of a man would quit a well-paying job as an engineer, throwing away a perfectly good career, to push a cab and dream about making chocolate, for crying out loud?" The thundering oration had been delivered in front of his mother, who had folded and refolded her hands, looking at her youngest child as if something had happened to his ability to think.

Answer him, she had mutely begged Keith, her eloquent eyes speaking for her.

"A man who marches to a different drummer," Keith had said mildly. He had long since ceased being affected by his father's displays of temper.

"Hogwash!" Richard Calloway had thundered.

"Thoreau," Keith had corrected.

His father had leveled a chilling glare at the woman he had been married to for over thirty-five years. "He gets it from your side of the family."

Keith had only smiled, then taken his leave. He had felt he owed it to his parents to tell them what he intended to do. He owed them the information, but not his life. Not anymore. His life was his own to do with as he pleased. And it pleased him to try something out of the ordinary.

He had done it the other way for too long. The awards in school had been for his father; even the degree had been earned to please him. But now Keith had taken stock of everything and decided that although his father was reasonably content with his achievements, Keith wasn't. He gained no satisfaction from the tedious tasks he had to perform day in, day out. He was bored with engineering. He refused to waste time any longer, watching a clock and aching to go home, just so he could go to sleep, then wake up in time to appear at his desk again the following morning.

His happiest times had been the summers when he was going to college. He had spent them working in the kitchen of Venus Chocolates. There he had been free to create, to get fully involved. He thought about those times often when the tedium of his job got to him.

It had all come to a head two months ago, when he had inherited an old two-story building on the outskirts of Manhattan from his grandfather. Life was issuing him a challenge, and he'd be damned if he was going to turn his back on it.

So he had quit his job, giving two weeks notice and champing at the bit until the time passed. He had taken a part-time job as a cabdriver so that he had some money coming in, then used his savings and the rest of his time to lay the foundations for his future. It was a future filled with risks that far outweighed the probability of success, but the risks invigorated him. Keith thrived on challenge. It made him feel alive. Working only part-time freed him to set the wheels in motion to make his dream a reality.

The building his grandfather had left him had a store on the ground floor, with two small apartments above it. One had been his grandfather's; the other had been occupied by the people who leased the store. Early Saturday morning he had discovered that the pair had departed, leaving most of their inventory and three months' unpaid rent in their wake. Keith had gone to work immediately. The store needed a great deal of renovation for what he had in mind. He couldn't afford to hire help, so he had to do everything but the wiring and plumbing himself. One day into the job and his expertise at carpentry was already being challenged. He loved it.

Today, though, he'd had no time for the store. He had agreed to take Ethan's shift in addition to his own. Ethan had come down with a roaring case of the flu and had begged him to take over.

Keith had been behind the wheel for ten hours now, taking time out only to grab a quick bite to eat. It had been at a coffee shop just the other side of the Fifty-ninth Street Bridge in Queens, and now he was starving.

He heard his stomach growl and heaved a grateful sigh that the off-duty sign was finally up overhead. Now all he had to do was make his way across town and bring the cab back in to the garage.

He rubbed the back of his neck. A shower was going to feel like heaven. It had been a scorcher. The temperature had dropped a little with the sun, but the air was still hot and humid. A cloudburst had been threatening all day but still hadn't materialized.

A quick flash of blond hair caught his attention as he turned the cab toward Fifty-third Street. But it was the accompanying scream that brought him to life. He came to a screeching halt and did a U-turn that he knew would have gladdened the heart of a policeman with a quota to fill, had one been watching.

Too many John Wayne movies, Keith admonished himself. He doubled back, his eyes straining to penetrate the shadows as he guided the cab down Fifty-third.

Teddi twisted and turned, trying desperately to free herself from the man's grasp. He had pounced quickly, and now he was dragging her deeper into the shadows of an empty storefront.

Not without a fight, he wasn't, she thought. With an effort she clamped her teeth down on the fleshy part of the man's hand. A howl of pain pierced the air. It was followed by a barrage of words she didn't understand.

Suddenly someone hurled her aside, pushing her out of the way. She stumbled backward, crashing into a garbage can and overturning it. A stray cat darted out from the shadows, as black as the night that had hidden it. It began pawing through the scattered contents of the garbage can as Teddi scrambled back to her feet.

Stunned, she tried to get a sense of what was going on. The man who had run to her rescue was grappling with the man who had grabbed her. She narrowed her eyes and focused on her assailant.

You're going to have to pick him out of a lineup, she told herself.

The mugger was as tall as her rescuer, but a lot thinner. A bandanna was wrapped around his dark head. A dirty undershirt contrasted with his olive complexion.

Teddi gasped involuntarily as she saw the gleam of a knife in the dull streetlight. Backing up, his eyes never leaving the other man, her assailant grabbed for the purse that had fallen from her shoulder.

"That's my purse!" Teddi cried.

"I figured that one out," snapped the stranger who had come to her rescue. He never even looked at her. He was too busy watching the other man.

"If I can't have the woman, I'll take a consolation prize," said the man in the bandanna.

"The hell you will!" Teddi looked around for something to hurl. She grabbed the garbage can lid and tossed it after the sprinting man like an oversize Frisbee. She nearly hit her rescuer, instead.

"The Mets could use you," he shot over his shoulder as he chased after the mugger.

A noise to her left made her jump. The cat, carrying something in its mouth, trotted by. Instinctively she took a step backward. "Welcome to New York City," she muttered, dragging her hand through her damp hair and pushing it out of her face.

For the second time in the space of ten minutes she felt a hand on her shoulder. This time Teddi doubled up her fist and swung as she turned. Her fist contacted a very lean, hard midsection.

Keith looked at her, amazement in his eyes. "Hey, why didn't you do that to him, Slugger?"

"I didn't get the chance," she retorted bitterly. She looked up into the stranger's eyes. They were dark and kind and filled with humor, despite the situation. "Did you get him?"

He gave a defeated sigh as he dropped his hands. "He got away."

Her heart sank. "And my purse?"

"With him."

She looked off into the shadows. "Damn!"

"That about covers the situation," he agreed. "Are you hurt?"

She frowned. "Just in my pocketbook."

"Could have been a lot worse." He didn't have to elaborate. "Is this yours?" He inclined his head toward the suitcase.

She nodded. "Yes."

"Well," he began as he picked up the suitcase and brushed it off for her, "at least he didn't get everything." He led the way back to the avenue.

"He might as well have," she said between clenched teeth. She stared off into the direction the mugger had taken. "All my money's in my purse."

"Traveler's checks, I hope."

She nodded. "Most of it."

"Copy down the serial numbers?"

"Of course I copied down the serial numbers," she retorted, still smarting over the incident. Her anger was directed at the mugger, but it spilled out onto the man next to her. She looked at him, an apology flashing in her eyes.

"You'd be surprised how many people don't. They forget to tell you that part in the commercials."

She smiled for the first time, liking his easy sense of humor. "I'm from Missouri, the Show Me State. We don't leave much to chance."

"Well, 'Missouri,' where were you off to before that unpleasant interlude?"

"To the Y on Eighth Avenue and Fiftieth Street."

He passed his hand over his face. "There *is* no Y on Eighth and Fiftieth. Not anymore, at any rate."

Teddi suppressed a sigh. "I found that out."

She tried not to sound disheartened, but he detected it anyway. He felt something nameless stir inside himself. He wanted, he realized, to cup her delicate face in his hands and kiss her. Long lashes swept along silken cheeks as she lowered her eyes, then looked up again. He felt the strong pull of desire.

"I'm sorry," she apologized suddenly. "I didn't even thank you for coming to my rescue."

"All in a day's work." He brushed her words off lightly.

She looked at him. He was dressed in a striped pullover that accented his muscular chest. Jeans completed the outfit. His dark brown hair brushed the top of his collar. "Are you an undercover policeman?" The comfortable small town she had come from had no need of undercover police. The four policemen who made up the force were always in full view, bored, for the most part, by the placid jobs they held.

"No," he answered. "A cabdriver."

It didn't make any sense. New Yorkers were supposed to be cold. "What?"

He laughed at the astonished look on her face. "Never mind." He led her over to his cab. He liked the way she raised her chin defiantly. Another woman might have dissolved into tears at a time like this. "Where can I take you?"

She looked at the sign. "You're off duty."

"I'm not. The cab is." He smiled and winked, sending a strange, electric sensation down her spine.

She thought of her purse, now in the hands of the mugger. "I can't pay you until I get reimbursed for my traveler's checks."

He shrugged away her protest. "We'll work something out."

Uh-oh, she thought. He was a smooth operator; she'd give him that. Teddi shook her head slowly. "I don't think so."

"Not very trusting, are you?"

She shook her head, her blond hair whipping across her cheek. "Nope."

"Should have thought of that before you put all your eggs in one basket."

"What?"

"Your money in your purse."

She wasn't sure if he was laughing at her or not, but her pride was stung anyway. "I didn't expect to be attacked."

"Nobody does," he said philosophically. He leaned against his cab, hooking his thumbs into his jeans. "Got any friends here? Besides me, I mean."

She forgot to hold back a smile at his words. She found herself liking him and wondering if it was wise. "No."

"What are you going to do?" He wondered how anyone in his right mind could have let a woman like this free to wander the streets of New York at this time of night. Didn't she have any family? A husband? He glanced at her left hand. Free. A boyfriend? He found himself hoping the answer to the last was no.

Teddi raised her chin. "I'll get by." She saw him cup his ear. "What are you doing?"

"Waiting to hear violins. This is New York, lady. Right now you've got no money and it's getting on toward evening."

He had her there. She didn't like not having any options, and it showed on her face. "Isn't there a mission or something you could take me to?"

He shrugged. "Not that I know of."

She felt at a loss for a moment. "Aren't you supposed to know these things?" she asked, frustrated. "What kind of a cabdriver are you?"

"The new kind. I haven't been at this long." He thought for a moment. "I could take you home."

He certainly didn't waste any time. "No, thanks." The look on her face told him exactly what she was thinking.

He held his hands up, protesting innocence. "It's aboveboard, really. I've got this extra apartment."

"Sure you do." Did he think she was born yesterday?

"No, really."

"What's a cabdriver doing with two apartments?" She told herself that she should just walk away, but after all, he *had* saved her life. She waited to hear him out.

"Trying to make them livable. They're not much, but it's better than sleeping in the park. Safer, too."

She had her doubts about that. As she contemplated her next move a fat raindrop landed on her nose. It was followed by another. And another. Within moments a torrential downpour had begun.

This was all she needed, she thought. To be drenched on top of everything else. What next? When was the plague of locusts coming?

Keith thought he had never seen anything so compellingly attractive as this woman with her blond hair plastered against her sensuous face. He wouldn't have been able to leave her out here even if it hadn't been raining. He took her arm and all but shoved her into the back seat of the cab.

"Look, I'm—" Teddi began to protest.

"A very stubborn woman. I saved you once this evening. I'm not going to follow you all night, fighting off potential muggers." He slammed the door on her.

He was acting as if he owned her. "Nobody asked you to," she pointed out.

He got in behind the wheel. Water was dripping down his face as he dragged his hand through his dark, wet hair. "That's beside the point. I'm an overgrown Boy Scout at heart."

Teddi crossed her arms over her soaked chest. Why was he showing such interest? she wondered. He didn't even know her. She thought of all the warnings she had heard in the past few days about New York City sharpies. Had she gone from the frying pan into the fire? "Somehow I don't think you want to show me your collection of knots."

"Lady, I'm hot, I'm tired, I've been pushing a cab for ten hours, and I just ran three blocks trying to save your purse. I'm too exhausted to try anything." He held up his hand as he turned around. "I swear to you the only reason I'm taking you with me is because I sat through *Saint Francis of Assisi* a dozen times when I was a kid."

She stared at him, totally confused. "What does that have to do with it?"

"He was kind to dumb animals."

Teddi clamped her mouth shut before her retort tumbled out.

Two

Teddi slid back against the cracked vinyl seat, trying to think. Twenty-four hours ago she had been in Willow Grove, Missouri, convincing her family that everything was going to be fine. Now here she was, a victim of a mugging, speeding off into the night with either the Angel Gabriel or Baby Face Nelson. Things were definitely not fine.

She studied the ID mounted on the dash. There was something comforting about his face, she decided. Something solid and reassuring. Besides, cabdrivers didn't kidnap people, she rationalized in an attempt to calm herself. She read his name, then murmured it out loud. Keith Calloway. Even his name sounded solid.

"Did you say something?" Keith asked, glancing at her in the rearview mirror.

His voice startled her. Embarrassed at being caught talking to herself, she blurted out the first thing that came to mind. "You haven't asked me my name."

"I was afraid you might bite my head off if I got that personal."

She let out a breath, chagrined. "I'm sorry. I guess I haven't been on my best behavior with you. But I've never been mugged before."

He grinned. She saw the way his eyes crinkled in the mirror. "That makes it a first for both of us. I've never saved anyone from a mugging before."

"Well, I'm glad you started with me."

The defensive edge was gone from her voice. What remained was melodic and soft. He wondered again how anyone so delicate-looking could have been allowed to come to New York without an armed guard. "So what is it?" he asked.

He caught her off guard again. "What?"

"Your name. What is it?"

She looked down at her hands. She saw that they were trembling slightly. The realization of what had almost happened to her was beginning to take hold. Calm, you've got to stay calm, she repeated to herself mentally. It's all over. You're safe. Maybe. "Teddi McKay."

"Teddie?" he asked. "As in bear?"

"No, as in Theodora."

He glanced into the rearview mirror and saw her wince as she said the name. "I can see why you'd lean toward a nickname. Personally, I would have used 'Dora.'"

She stared out blankly at the rain as it pelted the window next to her. "I had nothing to do with it. People have been calling me 'Teddi' ever since I can remember." She pushed a long strand of hair over her shoulder. "I suppose it had something to do with being the baby of the family, the one everyone held on their knee. I was the one they all cuddled."

"Like a teddy bear."

"Like a teddy bear," she finally agreed with a half smile. The city lights smeared into one another, highlighting the raindrops. The rhythmic beating of the windshield wipers and the distorted view of the city through the wet windows made her feel as if she were in a dream world, as if she would soon wake up and see that she was still in Willow Grove. It all seemed so unreal. Mugged after being in the city less than an hour. She wondered if that was some kind of record. "Shouldn't we go to the police?" she asked suddenly.

Keith cursed under his breath as he swerved in order to avoid being hit by a large truck speeding through a red light. "What did you say?"

"The police," she repeated. "Shouldn't I be talking to them?"

He didn't particularly feel like stopping and getting out in this weather. "I can take you to the precinct station," he told her reluctantly, "but I don't really think you're going to get much satisfaction."

"Well," she was willing to concede, "maybe not right away, of course, but eventually—"

"I don't think eventually has that many years in it."
He turned his head quickly in order to get a look at her
expression. Was she serious? "Missouri, you can't be
that naive."

"The word is optimistic," she corrected him tersely.

The set of his shoulders told her exactly what he
thought of her optimism. "If you say so." Under his
breath he muttered. "The word is hopeless."

He was beginning to live up to what she had heard
about New Yorkers. She refused to be daunted by his
pessimism. "I'd still like to talk to the police, please."

He shrugged. "If that'll make you happy." He
turned the cab neatly down the next street. "What are
you doing in New York, anyway?"

"I'm a dancer. I want to dance on Broadway."

Another hopeful. He thought of his brother-in-
law—his *ex*-brother-in-law—and the motley crew he
had brought to the house while he and Emily were
married. "Oh, well, that explains it."

She sensed an element of disdain in his voice. She
didn't like it. "Explains what?" she asked defensively.

"Why you were dumb enough to be wandering
around here alone at this hour of the night."

"I wasn't dumb," she retorted. "Besides, it was the
bus's fault."

"Would you like to explain that?"

"It broke down. I should have been here hours
ago," she said testily, struggling hard to remind herself that this man was her savior and, right now, the

only person she knew in the entire city. "What do you have against show people?"

Keith glanced at her as he came to a stop. The red light gleamed and shattered against the rain-splattered windshield. He couldn't help grinning at the defensive note in her voice. She looked rather adorable when she was angry, like an incensed pixie. "My sister married a would-be Sir Laurence Olivier. He did a lot of posing, a lot of brooding, and soaked her for twenty-five thousand dollars of my father's money before he left for parts unknown."

Teddi tossed her head, dismissing his story. She stared out the window. "We're not all like that," she snapped. She knew she shouldn't talk this way, not to the man who saved her from God-only-knew-what. It wasn't like her to be tactless or snippy. But she was tired, wet, shaken and more than a little bit frustrated. Her emotions had to be vented somehow.

The cab came to a halt. Was he tossing her out? As much as she had protested getting into the cab, the prospect of suddenly being on her own in this storm wasn't too pleasing.

Keith slung his arm around the back of the front seat and faced her. A dancer. From what he knew of the theater world, Teddi was going to be someone's hors d'oeuvre. She was just the type lecherous producers and directors preyed upon.

He saw uncertainty flicker in her eyes as they met his. Once again he felt a strong, protective pull toward her. When he was younger, his mother had lamented that he was forever bringing home strays. The same instinct that had moved him then moved him now.

"We're here," he announced.

"Where?" She stared out the window. It was hard to distinguish anything through the downpour.

"The police station."

"Oh."

He cocked his head. "Are you sure you won't change your mind about this? You're only going to be wasting your time."

She couldn't understand his reluctance to register a complaint. "If I don't report him, that guy's going to mug someone else."

He stared at her in disbelief. Just how sheltered was she? Keith leaned forward and pushed a strand of her hair away from her face. Even damp, it felt like silk to his fingertips. He felt the tiniest flicker of desire before it faded again. "You've been watching too many television shows where they catch they guy in an hour, minus commercials."

She straightened. "Just because I'm from Willow Grove—" she began indignantly.

"Willow Grove?" he echoed. The name made him think of a little town where everyone was related to everyone else and the county fair was the event of the year. She had no business being here.

He watched her perfectly shaped brows gather together in a scowl. "Something wrong with that?"

He shook his head. "You do get angry a lot, don't you?"

She sighed. He was right. She wouldn't blame him if he *did* turn her out. "It's my family."

"Your family?" he repeated. She had lost him.

She nodded. "No one else in my family has a temper." She shrugged, her palms turned upward. "I guess I got it all."

"Is your family all in Willow Grove?"

"Yes."

"But you're not."

"No." What was he driving at?

"Why?"

"I already told you. I want to be a dancer. On Broadway. I have dreams that can't possibly be realized in Willow Grove," she answered simply. "And I want to see what life's really all about."

Keith nodded, then stepped out of the cab. The rain was easing up, and the streets sparkled with a wet sheen. But the heat continued, made that much more unbearable by the humidity. He held the door open for her and offered her his hand.

She took it without hesitation, curling her fingers about his. His grip felt strong. He was someone who could keep her safe if she needed it, she thought, then smiled. She already had proof of that.

"C'mon." He motioned her away from the curb. She hurried with him toward a dilapidated building that looked as old as the city itself. Just the exterior made her feel depressed. He pulled open the heavy front door.

"This is the police station?" she asked incredulously, looking around.

A musty odor permeated the halls. There were large sections of the walls where the paint had peeled away, laying bare the plaster. The checkered linoleum on the floor had seen a generation of footsteps. She felt intimidated. The police station back in Willow Grove was a small room in the city hall. It was only six years old and smelled of flowers and after-shave lotion. This place smelled of despair.

"This is the police station," Keith confirmed. "Welcome to the real world."

She raised her chin defensively again, having gotten the distinct impression that he was laughing at her.

"Let's get this over with. I'm tired." There was no smile in his voice now. Before she could say anything he took her arm and ushered her over to the desk sergeant.

"Excuse me," Teddi said in a formal tone.

The bald, beefy-looking man behind the name plate Sergeant Gibson didn't appear to hear her and kept on writing.

Teddi rose up on her toes to make herself more imposing. "Excuse me."

The sergeant gave her a dismissive glance, then looked back to his work. "Be with you in a minute," he growled.

She turned to Keith. He seemed to be enjoying all this. "Are they always this rude?"

Keith nodded solemnly. "Always."

"Well, what is it?" the sergeant finally asked.

He sure was unfriendly, Teddi thought. "I'd like to report a mugging, please." She shifted uncomfortably. The sergeant gave her a very slow once-over. She was used to that. Teddi squared her slim shoulders.

Keith was reminded of a picture he had once seen of Joan of Arc as she faced the stake. Except that Saint Joan hadn't looked nearly this appealing.

"Whose?" Gibson's raised eyebrow met several furrows on his forehead.

"Mine," Teddi told him.

"You don't look any the worse for wear," the man commented candidly. "Couldn't have been much of a mugging."

Teddi felt her indignation flare. "He stole my purse, all my money!"

The higher her voice rose, the more disinterested the sergeant became. With a heavy sigh, as if this had happened merely to annoy him, he pulled out a clean sheet of paper. "All right, give me the details."

Teddi smiled in satisfaction as she gave Keith a sharp nod. There, her look seemed to say. Justice is going to prevail.

Keith crossed his arms over his chest and took a comfortable stance against the front desk. She was going to have to learn the hard way, it seemed.

Teddi went on talking animatedly for a full ten minutes, giving the desk sergeant much more information than he wanted. By the time she was finished not only did he have a description of the mugger, but he also knew the price of her bus ticket and what she had eaten for lunch.

With relief the sergeant finally put his pen down. Teddi stared at him, waiting. When he didn't say anything for a good thirty seconds, she prodded. "And?"

"And?" he asked, confused.

She gestured with her hand, as if to move him on to the next word. "And now what?" she finally asked.

"I file this." He waved the report in front of her.

That couldn't be all. "And?"

She was definitely getting on his nerves. "And I get a bicarbonate of soda to try to get rid of the taste of my wife's meat loaf."

The man was insufferable. "But I was *mugged*." Her indignant cry drew the attention of several of the officers milling about in the area.

"I know. You told me in vivid detail—on Fifty-third Street."

She braced her arms on the desk for emphasis. "Aren't you going to do anything about it?" she demanded.

Keith straightened slightly. He was going to have to get her out of here.

"Lady," Sergeant Gibson began wearily, "do you know how many purse snatchings there are in a day?"

"No." What did that have to do with it? "But—"

He wasn't about to let her get to the next word. "There is no 'but.' Less than two percent of the victims ever get their goods back—and by goods, I'm talking about the actual purse and maybe—just maybe—their IDs. You can kiss your money—"

"Traveler's checks," she interrupted stubbornly. "The least you can do is get the details right."

Keith saw the sergeant turning a unique shade of red. "Lady, you're just damned lucky that your purse is all you lost."

Teddi wasn't about to be pushed aside. "Just what kind of a policeman are you?"

"The kind that doesn't like to waste his time." His eyes shifted to Keith. "You," he growled, and Keith nodded in answer. "You a friend of hers?"

"After a fashion."

"Well, why don't you fashion her out of here?" he suggested. "And I'd tell her not to go strolling around Eighth Avenue next time."

Keith could see the anger rising in Teddi's blue eyes. "If this is the way New York's finest conduct business—" she began, only to feel Keith take a firm hold around her waist.

"I don't think you're making any points," he said in a low voice as he forcibly ushered her away from the desk sergeant.

"I don't want to make points." She craned her neck to see if the sergeant was actually just going to go on sitting there. He was. "I want to see justice done."

"If you don't watch your tongue you'll be seeing it done from inside a cell." He got her outside. Only when the door had closed behind them did he let go of her waist.

"He wouldn't arrest me."

"He could."

"On what charge?" she demanded.

"Public nuisance."

The rain had turned into a sprinkle now, misting against her face as she stood on the front stoop of the precinct. "I'm not a public nuisance. *He* is."

"But he has the badge."

He saw her shoulders sag a little as she gave in. "You were right."

He inclined his head. "Thank you."

"It was useless to come." Teddi bit her lip. "Doesn't anyone care in this city?"

He put his arm around her shoulders and pulled her a bit closer. It was strictly a friendly action. "Sure, lots of people do. Me, for instance." He looked down at her. Slowly he brushed away the wetness from her cheek. "My offer still holds, you know. You can stay in my spare apartment overnight—no strings attached."

"None?" It sounded too good to be true.

He held his free hand up as if he were taking an oath. "None."

She smiled, and he saw the gratitude flicker across her face. Suddenly, he wanted to trail his finger along the outline of her lips. "I guess I've been pretty awful about all this."

He moved his shoulders in a shrug. "Being new at the rescuing game, I couldn't say what standard behavior is like, but I *can* say that I've met more even-tempered women in my day."

She flushed. "I think I'd like to take you up on your offer."

He guided her to the cab without another word.

"Have you eaten?" he asked, sliding into the front seat. "I heard you mention lunch in your litany to the good sergeant, but you seemed to have skipped over dinner.''

''That's because I didn't have any.''

''I know a pizzeria that's open. Why don't I get a large pie to go?''

She felt her stomach suddenly tighten appreciatively. ''That sounds wonderfully normal.''

''Then pizza it is.'' He turned the cab in the general direction of the Fifty-ninth Street Bridge.

Teddi settled back and let out a long sigh. Tomorrow, she promised herself. Tomorrow things were going to be all right.

Keith stood there for a moment, holding the door open as he debated waking her or just taking her straight home and putting her to bed. Asleep she looked like the proverbial babe in the woods. No, more like some angel who had lost her way. He slid into the seat next to her and studied her for a moment. Disarmed of her frustration, she looked very young. He wondered how old she was. Twenty? Twenty-one? Ever so lightly, he touched her cheek. She stirred, but went on sleeping.

Are you going to regret this, Calloway? he asked himself. Not saving her. He would have done that for anyone. But was he going to regret taking her in? He had a feeling that, somehow, his life was going to be complicated by this stray.

He touched her shoulder, shaking her gently. ''With or without anchovies?''

Teddi stirred. She was having a nice dream and didn't want to let it go. ''Hmm?''

"Anchovies," he prodded. "On the pizza."

She sat up straight, trying to focus on her surroundings. "Oh, I must have fallen asleep."

"It looked that way from here." He smiled.

She felt at a disadvantage for a moment and shook her head to clear her thoughts. "What were you saying?"

"Do you want anchovies?"

"I don't know. I've never had any."

"Then you're in for a new experience. C'mon." He took her hand. "I'm not leaving you sitting out here alone."

Obediently she got out of the cab. Keith told himself to stop liking the sensation of having her around. This was all temporary. She'd be gone by morning.

Sal's Pizzeria was a small shop wedged in between a clothier's and a lingerie shop. It looked like a wakeful red eye, its canopy a brightly striped red and white, its well-lit window a gleaming beacon. Inside there were only two customers: a couple busy arguing. Keith hustled Teddi to the counter. A friendly-looking curly, dark-haired man with a splattered apron turned around from the oven.

"Hey, Keith, what're you doing out so lat...?" Sal's voice trailed off as he looked at Teddi. A broad grin surfaced as he wiped his hands. "I think I might take up driving a cab myself."

"We'd like a pizza, Sal," Keith told him.

Sal's eyes were still on Teddi. His wide smile put her at ease. "What kind?" he asked her.

"Large," she answered.

Keith laughed. Teddi looked up at him. She liked the sound of his laugh. It was deep and hearty and made her feel warm. "Make it with everything," he instructed his friend.

"One kitchen sink coming up," Sal promised.

"Do you come here often?" Teddi asked.

Keith leaned against the counter. "Only when I'm hungry."

"You don't cook?" she asked.

"Only when I have to."

She nodded. That was the way she felt about cooking. Her mother and sisters had always been after her to learn, but she had always preferred to spend the time practicing her dance routines. "I'll pay for half," she volunteered.

"I'll put it on your tab," he answered.

"Oh." For a moment she had forgotten that she had no money. The memory brought a frown to her face.

"Hey," Keith said, brushing his knuckles against her cheek. He smoothed the frown away. "I thought we'd gotten past that."

"Sorry."

"You say that a lot, you know."

"I know," she murmured.

As the bright light played on her silky silver-blond hair, Keith once again got a very definite quickening sensation in the pit of his stomach. Once again he had the feeling that his life wasn't ever going to be the same again.

Three

———

I want you to know that it was very hard to resist the temptation,'' Teddi informed Keith as she slid out of the cab.

He looked appreciatively at her long legs as she swung them out. She was confusing him again. He had only been with her a little more than an hour and already he was beginning to suspect that being in a mild state of confusion around her was the norm. A rather sexy smile rose to his lips. "Oh?" He walked to a darkened storefront. There were metal bars across the window, and strange objects hung inside it.

This wasn't what she had envisioned. She had been overly optimistic again, Teddi thought. "It took all my willpower not to steal a bite."

He glanced at her over his shoulder. "Oh, you're talking about the pizza."

She gave him a quizzical look. "Of course I'm talking about the pizza. What did you think I was talking about?"

"Me," he teased as he juggled the large pizza box while fishing in his pants pocket for his keys. "I thought maybe you wanted to have your way with me in the cab." He unlocked a door next to the storefront. "After you." He held the door open.

Hesitantly she walked into the dark foyer, her suitcase in tow. Was he joking or not? "Um, Keith, I think we'd better get something straight."

"Oh?" The word was couched in innocence. He began to climb the long, dark stairway.

Teddi gripped the chipped banister and followed. "Yes. I'm not that kind of...a woman." Damn, she had almost said "girl." Teddi bit her lip. Everyone back home was always referring to her as a girl. She wasn't a girl any longer. She was a woman. Being twenty-one made her one, even if she hadn't experienced everything some women had. She would. Someday.

"What kind of woman is that?" He stopped on the landing and turned around to face her. His body was a hairbreadth away from hers on the small landing where the stairs came to a dead end, with an apartment to either side. Teddi was aware of a flicker of heat between them, and it had nothing to do with the oppressive weather.

She moistened her lips. Usually it was easy for her to put men who came on to her in their proper place. This time she found herself fumbling for words. "The kind who repays favors with—with favors."

He ran a finger along her cheek. "You're a heartless woman, Missouri." He turned and unlocked the door to the left.

"It's not that I'm not grateful," she explained, following him in. "I'm just not grateful in *that* way. Oh." She bumped into him. "Did I hit the pizza?"

"Nice of you to inquire. No, but you got my toe." Teddi felt the strong outline of his body. An instant later she felt her pulse accelerate. "You can get off it anytime you like," he prodded.

Teddi took a self-conscious step back. For just a moment her body had tingled in quite an uncustomary way. She cleared her throat. "Don't you have any lights in here?"

"Not when I'm out." He put the pizza down and reached behind her.

She thought he was cornering her against the wall. "Hey, I thought I told you that I'm—"

"Not that kind of woman," he completed tolerantly. "Yes, I know. But whatever kind of a woman you are, you're standing in front of the light switch."

"Oh." She laughed at her own overreaction and stepped aside.

Her warmth radiated against his skin as she brushed by him. He felt an insistent stirring, hot and tight, in the pit of his stomach. He gave in to the overwhelming impulse that held him in its grip.

"Still," she heard him say, "there is something to be said about the dark."

A moment later she felt his hands on her shoulders as if to steady her. Or himself. Whichever it was, the next thing she knew, he had lowered his head. She felt his breath on her lips just before he touched them with his own.

Teddi didn't move. It was as if she were paralyzed. Just the slightest pressure from his mouth and all her senses stood at attention, waiting for what was to come next, apprehensive and anticipatory at the same time.

His kiss was meant to be light and affectionate, and that was how it started. Had she pulled back, he would have stopped. But she didn't pull back. Instead, she let him kiss her. In fact, she kissed him back. The suitcase that she had carried up from the cab fell to the ground. She buried her hands in his hair. A wild drumming in her ears reflected the tempo taken by her heart, and her pulse broke the sound barrier.

Keith had to restrain himself from deepening the kiss. Her lips were the most delicious thing he had ever tasted. A man could get drunk on them, he thought, his mind cloudy. His own breath quickened. With a supreme effort he ended the kiss, his forehead against hers.

They were both silent, attempting to regain their composures, bewildered by the flash of lightning that had passed between them.

"Missouri, you're the sweetest thing I've ever sampled, which is saying quite a lot."

Teddi straightened, the misty mood shattered. The man was actually bragging about how many women he had had. "Oh, you're one of those." Into the frying pan, that was where she had jumped, she told herself.

"One of what?"

She shrugged as she searched for the right word. "A womanizer, a Romeo."

He laughed. The image tickled him. While his love life had been satisfying, he had never thought of himself in quite that way.

"No, but I've had a lot of different kinds of chocolate. And, like I said, you taste sweeter than anything I've ever tasted."

He switched on the light. It took her several seconds to adapt to the brightness. She looked around. There was a lot to be learned about a man from his apartment. They were standing in the living room. A dark brown shag rug covered the entire floor. The furnishings weren't modern but had a look of comfort and warmth. She liked the place immediately. It belonged to a man who was comfortable in his surroundings, a man at ease with himself. It heartened her. "Are you a—what do you call it?—chocoholic?"

"No," he corrected. "A chocolatier."

"Sounds like mousketeer," she commented. "Just exactly what is a chocolatier?"

She followed as he carried the pizza into the kitchen and put it on the table. He opened the cupboard and took out two large plates. "Someone who makes chocolate." He pushed a plate toward her.

That image didn't fit him in the slightest. She could far more readily accept the fact that he was an out-of-work actor pushing a cab and waiting for his break than someone who made chocolate. Then she remembered his comment about the theater. He was far more complex than he seemed, she decided. "You make chocolate?"

"Yep." He handed her a knife and fork. Teddi placed them next to her plate, then promptly ignored them.

"What a strange hobby for a man."

"It's not a hobby." He opened the box, and the aroma of pizza filled the room. Teddi looked at it hungrily. "Making chocolate's going to be my career." He cut a piece for her, and she took it quickly and bit into it with delighted abandon, eschewing utensils. "There's more," he told her, amused.

She glanced up and smiled, still chewing. "Do you really make chocolate?"

He pulled napkins out from another cupboard and dropped a handful on the table. "Why is that so hard to believe?"

She shrugged, taking another bite. Keith pushed a napkin toward her, then lifted a piece of pizza onto the plate in front of him.

"I've never met anyone who made chocolate before," she told him honestly. "I mean, my mother and sisters were always canning anything they could get their hands on, but nobody ever made chocolate." She took another bite. "Do you make it from scratch?"

"From an itch." He made no effort to hide his amusement. She was delightful in a very disturbing way.

"Do you have any around?"

He held his hand up as he tried to find the end of a long string of mozzarella. "It doesn't go with pizza."

"It's edible, isn't it?"

He put down his fork. "Is that your only criterion?"

"Yes." She grinned. "I like to eat."

She certainly didn't look it. It was his first warning that she had a metabolism that turned everything to pure energy, but he was too enchanted to pay proper attention.

Keith looked at her open, innocent face, then pushed himself away from the table. He went over to the cupboard and opened it. Six mugs with a variety of sayings hung in a neat row, overseeing a blue-and-white tin that had once held an assortment of Danish cookies. He hesitated for a moment. He usually saved his samples for business. Making up his mind, he pulled the container out, then placed it on the table in front of her and took off the lid.

"I suggest you don't eat them together." He nodded at the pizza that had all but vanished from her plate.

Teddi finished the last bite and asked, "May I?"

"Sure." He gestured toward the tin.

It was filled with chocolate in the shape of angels. She picked one up and took it out. Keith watched as she took a tiny bite of the wing. Her eyes opened wide in delighted surprise. "Mmm." Teddi nodded vigorously.

She was just a stranger he had met, but for some reason her approval pleased him far more than it should have. "I take it that's a compliment."

"This is really good." She took a closer look at the man straddling the chair opposite her, fascinated. "What do you call it?"

His brows drew together. What an odd question. "Chocolate."

She shook her head. "No, no, I mean commercially. Everything's got to have a name."

"How about Felix?"

She frowned as she eagerly took another bite. "You're not being serious."

"You noticed."

"If you're going to market it, it has to have a catchy name." She finished it. It was heavenly. "There's a lot of competition out there."

He hadn't thought about a name. He had been too caught up in perfecting the formula, securing the right cocoa beans and, just lately, in ordering the necessary equipment for large-scale production. "All right, how does Keith's Kandy sound?"

She shook her head. "Too blah."

"Thanks a lot."

She turned another angel over in her hand, thinking. "She looks like she's sleeping."

"Maybe she finds the name Keith's Kandy blah, too."

But Teddi wasn't listening. "How about Chocolate Dreams?"

"Sounds good to me." He rose, taking the tin with him. "Ten years from now, when you come across a box of Chocolate Dreams, you'll have the honor of knowing you named it." He put the tin back in its place and closed the cupboard door. He had a feeling that if he left the tin out she'd eat all the angels.

He turned around to see her taking another slice of pizza. Where was she putting all this? "You always pick at your food like that?" he asked, amused.

"Can't seem to stop once I'm started. You're not eating," she said, apparently just having noticed.

"I'm getting full just watching you." He sat down again. The light in the tiny kitchen was reflecting off her hair, and he curled his fingers into his palms to keep from reaching out and stroking her head. You've got no business thinking about her like that, he told himself. You don't need any complications in your life, remember? He turned his attention away from the ethereal woman at his table and to his meal.

"You're actually going to wait that long?"

He jerked his head up. "What?"

Didn't he pay attention to what he said? she wondered. "Ten years. Are you going to wait that long before you market it?"

Her enthusiasm tickled him. She was the type of person, he had no doubt, who saw everything as being simple. "You shouldn't talk with your mouth full, you know."

She gave a slight shrug. "Can't be helped. Thoughts keep crowding into my head."

The way she jumped from one topic to another, it must be a tight squeeze in there, he thought.

She waited until she had swallowed another bite, then went on. "What's wrong with now?"

"For what?" He wondered if anyone had ever gauged the speed of her mind.

"For marketing your chocolate," she said impatiently.

"Nothing's wrong with now except that I haven't got the facilities ready yet. I'm remodeling the store downstairs to accommodate the necessary equipment."

"How long will that take?" She separated yet another slice from the remaining pizza.

He propped his head up on his hand. "Anyone ever tell you that you're nosy?"

"Yes."

He grinned. "Just so long as you know."

"So?" she prodded him. "How long will it take you?"

"Until it's finished." He winked, pretending to be mysterious.

Keith moved his chair a little closer to Teddi. He found that he liked talking to her. Nobody had ever taken his dream of being a chocolatier seriously. His family and friends had always expected great things of him when he was in school. No one, he thought with a wry smile, had ever expected chocolate.

"How does a cabdriver come to own two separate apartments and a store?" she asked, debating whether to take another slice, then deciding against it.

"Oh, c'mon," he prodded. "There's still half a pie left."

She shook her head, her eyes twinkling. "No, I've had enough. You can have the rest tomorrow. For breakfast."

The thought of pizza for breakfast didn't sit well with his stomach. Hers, he had no doubt, was probably cast iron. He let the lid flop down over the remainder of the pizza.

"You didn't answer my question."

He put his hand to his head, massaging his brow. "Probably because I'm feeling a little overwhelmed. Which question are you referring to?"

She tilted her head and repeated her question patiently. The man's mind obviously wandered a lot, she thought. "Why do you have two apartments and a store?"

"My grandfather left them to me." He nodded at the apartment in general. "He used to live here."

Teddi looked around. That explained the warm feeling she had gotten when she walked into the room. "Did you live here with him?"

"No. I had an apartment on the Island. Long Island," he clarified when she looked at him, puzzled. "Near where I worked."

"Which was?"

"At Condor Aerospace. You know, you ask an awful lot of questions for someone from the Midwest, Missouri."

"Which is why I'm here. The pace there was too slow for me."

"I think the pace anywhere would be too slow for you. I don't think I've ever met anyone quite like you."

She smiled, and a dimple formed near the right-hand corner of her mouth. "Is that a compliment or a complaint?"

"I'm not sure yet."

She continued, undaunted. "You're an engineer?"

"Was," he corrected her.

"And you gave it up to drive a cab and make chocolate?"

"That about sums it up." He waited for the inevitable why. Everyone else had hit him with it.

Instead she just nodded. Her expression told him that she understood. "I think that's wonderful." She saw his brow lift slightly. "You're surprised, aren't you?"

"A little."

"I'll bet your family doesn't approve."

"No."

She empathized entirely. It made her feel good to have something in common with him. Vaguely she wondered why. "Mine either. They wanted me to stay where I was and marry Willard."

The name captured his attention. "Willard?"

Teddi dragged her hand through her hair. It felt as if it weighed a ton from absorbing all the moisture in the air. As Keith watched she braided the thick blond mane into a single plait. "Willard Wilson."

He didn't know why, but for just a moment he felt quite resentful of Willard, whoever he was. He squelched the absurd feeling. "Your boyfriend?"

"Everyone else thought so."

"What did you think?"

She leaned back, nudging the long braid over her shoulder. He thought of Rapunzel. "I thought about dancing, about leaving Willow Grove," she confessed.

"How old are you, Missouri?" he asked.

She lifted her chin a little. "Old enough."

"For what?" he teased. He couldn't resist the temptation of touching her. He covered her hand with his.

A warm feeling spilled through her, and for a moment she left her hand where it was. "For everything that I want to do." She looked at the plates on the table. "Need any help with the dishes?" she offered.

He rose and picked up the two plates. "I rarely wash paper plates."

The plastic coating and flowered design had fooled her. She felt a little silly. The feeling didn't last.

"Want to see your apartment?" he suggested.

Her apartment. It had a nice ring to it, she thought. After having shared a room with her sister all her life, having a place of her own, no matter how temporary, sounded wonderful.

"Sure." She was on her feet instantly, following him out into the dim hallway. She watched him dig into his pocket and take out a key, then open the door. A musty smell greeted her nose, and she wrinkled it slightly.

"Do you have another?" she asked.

Even in the dark, the apartment had a dinginess that was hard to shake. Did she really expect him to offer her an alternative? he thought. "Apartment?" he asked.

"No, key." She nodded at the one in his hand.

She's afraid I'm going to walk in on her while she's asleep, he thought. "No," he lied. "This is the only one." There was no need to tell her that he had a duplicate. He wasn't about to use it unless she screamed fire in the middle of the night.

He reached past her and switched on the light. The naked bulb overhead illuminated a medium-size room that was littered with boxes, dust and furniture that had gone past the word "dilapidated" several years ago.

"It looked better in the dark," she said, walking in. A spider scurried over her foot and disappeared into a crack in the wooden floor.

"It needs a little work."

"It needs a demolition crew." She ran her hand over the kitchen table; it came away sticky. Had someone actually *lived* here like this?

"There's always my place." He nodded back toward the hallway.

"I'll make do," she said quickly. "Is there a bed around?" If there was, she didn't see it.

"The couch folds out," he told her.

She looked at the sofa against the wall. It was a washed-out shade of brown. Three of the buttons were missing from the cushions, and it sagged badly in the center. "Are you sure?"

He nodded. "I'll get you some clean sheets and towels," he offered.

She sniffed the stale air. "Some disinfectant wouldn't be out of line, either," she said under her breath. She marched over to the window and tried to open it. It was stuck. "Who lived here?"

"The people who used to lease the store downstairs." Keith came up behind her and gripped the window sash. She saw the muscles in his forearms strain as he pushed the window up. "There, fresh air, such as it is," he said, turning to her.

For a moment she thought he was going to kiss her again. She knew she wasn't ready for that, so she moved away. Absently she walked over to one of the boxes. A false nose with glasses lay on top of the haphazard heap of things inside. She picked it up. "What did they do?"

"Sold gag gifts."

She let the glasses drop back on the pile. "Not too often, I take it."

"That's why they left . . . suddenly."

A few minutes later he left her with a set of sheets and some navy blue towels that reminded her of his eyes.

She looked around. "Well, Teddi, you've been in worse places—but for the life of me, I can't remember when."

She set about making the sofa into a bed and then collapsed on what passed for a mattress.

Fifteen minutes later she realized that it was no use. She couldn't sleep. Not here. Not like this. She wasn't a fanatic about cleanliness, but sleeping in the city dump was quite another matter. She got out of bed and slipped on a light robe over her short nightgown. Restless, she prowled the small apartment, looking for something to clean with. It didn't surprise her when she didn't find anything.

She looked at the wall that separated the two apartments. Maybe he wasn't asleep yet, she thought, opening the front door. She stepped out into the hall. A sliver of light was showing beneath his door. She hesitated only a second, then knocked.

The door opened almost immediately, and the words she had meant to say disappeared. He was standing in the doorway, wearing only pajama bottoms that hung low on his taut hips. His muscular chest was hazed with light brown hair, swirling down until it almost formed an arrow below his navel. As a dancer she was used to well-built men, but she had never run into anyone as attractive as he was. She forced her gaze to his face.

There wasn't very much to her nightgown, Keith thought, but there seemed to be an awful lot more to her than he had first suspected. He felt his pulse quickening as he took in the swell of her breasts beneath the thin fabric. He reached out and closed her robe, which had slipped open. "For a woman who doesn't want trouble," he told her, shaking his head, "you certainly do invite it. Every man has his breaking point, Missouri. Let's not test mine."

She was touched by the gesture.

"Now—" he ran his hand through his tousled hair "—what's the matter?"

"Do you have a broom?"

He stared at her. "Isn't two in the morning a little early to take inventory?"

"The apartment's a little messy—"

"The apartment's a lot messy," he corrected her. "But—"

"And I can't sleep," she went on, as if he hadn't said anything, "so I thought I'd clean it for you."

He thought of arguing with her, but he instinctively knew he'd come up the loser. "Wait here," he instructed. "I'll see what I can do."

She leaned against the door, watching the muscles in his back ripple as he walked away from her. Her chest tightened, and she had to think about breathing.

"I don't have a broom," he called from the depths of his walk-in closet. "Just a vacuum cleaner."

"Even better," she said.

He brought it out to her. "All yours." He scotched the idea of carrying it into the other apartment for her. The more distance between them when she was wearing next to the nothing, the better. "You don't have to do this, you know."

"Yes, I do," she said, giving him the most bewitchingly determined smile he had ever seen. Then she left, Hoover in hand.

Keith sighed, then closed the door. Life had certainly gotten more interesting in the past few hours.

Four

Keith lay on his bed, his fingers laced together under his head as he stared at a spot on the ceiling. The droning hum of his vacuum cleaner was keeping him awake. He sighed. No, it wasn't the vacuum cleaner keeping him awake. It was the person pushing it around who was preying on his mind.

She had asked so many questions he had never gotten the chance to find out very much about her. With the limited information he had, he was attempting to figure out what it was about her that intrigued him. Keith closed his eyes, moving restlessly. He kicked at the covers, bunching them at the foot of the bed. He wasn't supposed to be wasting time trying to figure her out. She would be gone by morning. Noon at the latest. There was no reason for him to lie there recreating her blond softness in his mind's eye. She was just a woman he had run into. Nothing more.

He rolled over and told himself that he wasn't going to be worth a damn in the morning if he didn't get some sleep. He had always been able to concentrate with an astounding single-mindedness on whatever he wanted to accomplish, so why couldn't he free his mind of her? It shouldn't be so difficult.

If only the noise would stop.

When it did, several minutes later, he raised his head from the pillow, anticipating the sound of her footsteps. He fully expected her to come bursting in with another absurd request. When nothing but the sound of a passing car broke the silence he let his head fall back against the pillow. The clock on the nightstand read two-thirty. If he was lucky and fell asleep in the next three seconds, he thought with mounting despair, he'd manage to get five hours' sleep before he had to be on his feet again.

Teddi shoved the vacuum cleaner into a corner. She had captured every bit of dust she possibly could. She looked around, her hands on her slender hips. It didn't look any better vacuumed, just cleaner.

"What would help is a fairy godmother with a magic wand, or a charge card to Macy's," she muttered, pushing her bangs out of her eyes. She had taken off her robe when she had started vacuuming, because the place was so hot. The window that Keith

had opened only admitted the city dirt and noise.
There was no relief from the heat.

She moved to the window, willing a breeze to rise.
None came to greet her. Didn't the noise ever stop? she
wondered, looking out. Across the street she saw a
couple walking arm in arm, oblivious to the time. A
bus went by, traveling in the opposite direction, several passengers on board. What a change from back
home, she thought. Buses there stopped running at
ten. A smile played across her lips. This was what she
wanted, a change. That, and opportunity.

She glanced to her left at the wall that separated the
two apartments. He had certainly come along at the
most opportune time, she thought. If he hadn't come
when he had . . . She let the thought go.

Looking down at her hands, she saw that they were
dirty. Sighing, she went to the sink and washed up.
With new determination she turned her attention to
the half-dozen boxes scattered around the room. She
lined them up against the far wall, piling all sorts of
nonsensical gag items into them. Slowly things began
to take shape. And as they did, so did her plans.

Why should she go hunting for an apartment when
this one was available? It wasn't exactly what she had
envisioned, not even at her most pessimistic, but even
the fact that it was so tiny and neglected had a good
side to it. She was certain that Keith wouldn't charge
her very much. Not for a place like this. She surveyed
the room. It looked larger now that the boxes were
piled against the wall. With a few touches here and
there it could look homey in time. After all, his

apartment did, and it wasn't that much different from this one.

A moth-eaten towel lay on the side of the sink. She dampened it and began cleaning the kitchen table. At her efforts, a lighter color began to emerge. Her motions slowed as her thoughts absently returned to Keith. He hadn't tried to take advantage of her. Not really. And that was good, too. The kiss in his apartment had been . . . pleasant. More than pleasant. Interesting. She smiled broadly. She was going to stay.

A movement in the corner by the refrigerator caught her eye. She dropped the cloth and grabbed the abandoned vacuum cleaner hose.

Keith was just falling asleep when he heard the crash. He bolted upright. What? He remembered Teddi as his feet hit the floor. He threw open the drawer of his nightstand, grabbed the other key to the apartment across the hall and hurried out the door. He was in her apartment before his eyes were fully focused. He found her standing in the middle of the room, holding the vacuum cleaner hose aloft like a weapon.

"What the—"

Teddi turned, surprised to see him. "You have mice," she announced. There was no fear in her voice. "You're going to have to do something about them before I sign the lease."

He blinked twice, trying to get not only his eyes but the situation into focus. "What lease?"

"Mine," she said brightly. "For the apartment," she clarified when it became obvious he didn't understand what she was talking about. "I've decided to stay." Her eyes widened as she fully comprehended the meaning of his presence. "Wait a minute. How did you get in here?"

He nodded behind him. "Through the door."

"But I locked it," she protested as he came toward her. "You said you didn't have another key."

He took the vacuum cleaner out of her hands. "I lied."

Having disarmed her, he turned around and removed himself and the vacuum cleaner from the room. "See you in the morning."

He wasn't even going to consider what had just transpired, he told himself, not until he could think clearly. The sight of her standing there with the glare from the bulb overhead highlighting her sleek, inviting curves was not conducive to clear thinking of any sort. Besides, she had a delivery that rivaled automatic weapon fire. At the moment, he was no match for her.

Just before he finally dropped off to sleep for the second time that night, he began to think that maybe he should have taken a different route home.

Teddi felt as if she had just drifted off to sleep, when she heard knocking. She had just gotten accustomed to the sound of the cars outside her window instead of sparrows. The knocking disoriented her. Her lids lay heavy on her eyes. Daylight seeped in beneath her lashes.

"Mmm?"

"Open the door, Missouri."

She jerked her head up. Last night, the mugging, the police station, Keith in his pajamas, all crowded into her head at once. "Coming," she called.

She dragged her hand through her hair as she unlocked the door and pulled it open. "Why didn't you use your key?" she asked, still annoyed that he had lied to her.

"That's only for emergencies—like fire, earthquakes and mice." He looked down at her. The by now familiar tightness in his stomach hit him again. Why didn't she wear her damn robe? He stifled a desire to pull her into his arms. "Get dressed and come over for breakfast." His voice was deceptively nonchalant, hiding the desire that he felt.

The door to his apartment was open, and she could smell the strong aromas of fresh coffee and bacon sizzling on the skillet.

"I'll be right there," she promised, then closed the door to her apartment.

Within five minutes she was out of the shower, her skin tingling from the vigorous scrubbing she had given it. She felt the muscles in her shoulders protesting as she raised her arms to comb her hair. The early-morning cleaning spree and relatively sleepless night were demanding their fee. She contemplated exercising for a few minutes in order to limber up, but the memory of the smell of bacon and coffee proved insurmountable. She succumbed to temptation.

In deference to the weather she tied her hair into a ponytail and put on forest-green culottes topped with a light green pullover. After slipping on low-heeled sandals she was ready to meet the world. Or at least breakfast.

The door to Keith's apartment was unlocked. "Hi," she called out as she entered.

"Over here." He glanced in her direction. She looked like a fresh-faced ingenue out of some forties comedy, he thought. *A Date with Judy* or *Meet Corliss Archer*. She was definitely going to need protection against the wolves out there.

He cut himself short. He had no business butting in. Twenty-four hours ago he hadn't known she existed. She was a big girl, and her life was her own. And he, he reminded himself, had a business to establish and a cab to push. That left very little time to play guardian angel, especially since the thoughts that were going through his mind were anything but angelic.

That was another thing he didn't have time for. Involvements were something to be considered later, once his business was on its feet. At the moment he had no time to work at a relationship—especially with someone who was interested in theater! Their temperaments were undoubtedly poles apart.

But sometimes, the thought sailed through his mind, relationships worked at themselves.

She walked in and stood behind him. He could smell a mixture of soap and a fresh, clean scent that seemed to be hers alone. Something like wild flowers, he thought. Unmistakably sweet and undeniably sensual.

Teddi cocked her head and looked hungrily at the bacon and scrambled eggs on the stove. "I thought you couldn't cook."

"The word isn't 'couldn't,'" he said, laying strips of bacon on a paper towel. "It's 'wouldn't.' Normally. Once in a while the spirit moves me."

"Like this morning?" she asked cheerfully.

"Like this morning." Gingerly he transferred the bacon to a plate. "The thought of pizza for breakfast was rather unappetizing."

"I can eat anything."

"I had a hunch."

She looked around hopefully. "Can I do anything to help?"

You could try not standing so close to me, he thought. "No, just take your appetite over to the table." He divided the eggs and bacon between the two plates.

She looked down as he placed her plate in front of her. "What, no paper plates?" she asked.

"Special occasion." She looked at him quizzically. "Your first morning in New York."

"Which might not have happened if not for you." The smile she gave him was soft, but there was determination in her eyes. He would bet that she was a woman who knew her own mind. He was surprised when she put her hand on his as he sat down, squeezing lightly. Warmth traveled up his arm. "I can't thank you enough."

It was a decided change from the effervescent woman at his table last night and the angry firebrand at the police station. "Cleaning the apartment is thanks enough," he said dismissively, embarrassed by her words.

"I had to clean it," she told him simply. With an easy movement she picked up a forkful of scrambled eggs. "I can't live in a pigsty."

"About living..." he began. He wasn't at all sure that it would be a good idea to have her around at this point in his life. She was definitely a distraction at a time when he couldn't afford any.

She drew a breath and pressed her lips together in a frown. It wasn't annoyance. She was thinking. "I hope you're not going to charge too much rent. After all, it's a tiny place." Ignoring the astonished look in his eyes, she rolled right over him. "And I hope you extend credit, because until I get my traveler's checks refunded I don't have any money to give you. Besides, you have to admit—"

He held up his hand before she could go on—and he had no doubt that she could go on and on and on. "Why don't we just eat breakfast first and then work out the details?" he heard himself saying. It was incredible. Just a few minutes ago he had been planning to turn her down. She was distracting him already.

"I can do both."

"But I can't."

She accepted that with a careless shrug and immediately moved on to something else. "Where did you learn to cook?" Her father had known that bread belonged in the toaster if you wanted toast, but that was the extent of his culinary abilities, which had suited him just fine. He had been of the old school, believing that men were supposed to earn a living and women were supposed to cook—with a few fringe benefits thrown in for both.

"Elise taught me?"

"Your girlfriend?"

"Our cook."

The revelation surprised her. "You had a cook?"

He nodded. "And a maid."

"And you're satisfied living here?" she marveled.

"They weren't really mine." He chuckled. "They worked for my parents. And living here suits me fine. Elise introduced me to making chocolate."

Teddi looked interested, so he continued with his story. "Every Sunday morning she got up early to make a whole batch of French pastries for the family. I loved chocolate, so she always made something with chocolate in it. She let me hang around and watch. One day I asked her how chocolate was made, so she bought me a book about it. It was meant for adults, and I was about eight at the time, but she seemed to think I was equal to it." He smiled fondly, thinking of the mornings he had spent plying her with endless questions she had never grown tired of answering.

Teddi saw his square jaw soften. He had been attached to Elise, she guessed. She liked knowing that about him.

"Elise was the only one who ever had time to answer any questions." A pat of butter melted on his toast. "I guess she was lonely. She never had any family of her own."

"I can't imagine what it would be like not to always have someone around," Teddi admitted. She nibbled on her last strip of bacon. "My problem's always been the opposite. No space of my own."

"Your own space can sometimes be very lonely," he told her.

She studied him. Long, dark lashes framed his eyes as he looked down at his plate. Had he been lonely, too, like Elise? she wondered. "But you had a sister," she recalled.

"And two brothers," he added matter-of-factly.

"And you were still lonely?"

He would have liked to drop the subject, but found himself answering her, instead. "We didn't exactly get along. We were like six strangers living under the same roof, with a common surname tying us together."

She thought of slumber parties, secrets whispered in the middle of the night under tented blankets, trips to the fair, boisterous mealtimes, and her heart went out to him. "Oh, I'm sorry."

He roused himself, wondering what it was about her that caused him to tell her things he normally never allowed to surface. Abruptly he changed the topic. "Do you really want to lease the apartment?"

Excitement glowed in her eyes. "Absolutely."

He was going to regret this, he told himself. "I can let you have it for three-fifty a month."

She nearly choked on her toast. "Three *hundred* fifty? For *that*?" Her eyes were wide. "How about if I keep the mice? Will it be less then?"

Not only was she making him do something against his better judgment, but she was arguing with him about the price. He eyed her carefully. "All right, how much were you thinking of spending?"

She gave it very little thought. "Two hundred."

"A month?" he asked incredulously.

She nodded.

"Nothing goes for two hundred dollars a month in New York unless you're renting a pup tent in Central Park."

"What about your store?"

"That's not for rent."

"No." She folded her napkin into a tiny square, then smoothed it out carefully as she talked. "I mean, you said last night that you were getting it into shape."

"Yes?" What was she up to? He watched the early-morning sun diffusing through her hair, then forced his mind back to the apartment he didn't really want to rent out.

"Why don't I help you in my spare time?"

"Help me do what?"

"Clean it."

He dismissed the suggestion. "It needs more than that."

"I'll do whatever you need," she said eagerly. "Look, it's only temporary. Once I get a job as a dancer I can pay you more, but right now I don't have much money available."

He was losing ground, and he knew it. What was worse, he didn't seem to mind anymore. "And how much *do* you have?"

"Not much," she confessed. "I was counting on getting work pretty fast."

Hadn't anyone stopped to tell this innocent the facts of life before letting her board the bus? "Not much of a realist, are you?" He shook his head. "It seems to be a common failing of you artsy types. You don't think things through."

"This from a man who gave up a maid, a cook and a job as an engineer to live over a store and make chocolate angels?"

One of the things Keith prided himself on was knowing when he was licked. "You've made your point." What the hell? It *was* only temporary. She'd probably leave for fancier quarters as soon as she found something. And in the interim he *could* use some help getting the store into shape. He could make the most of the deal. Besides, he had a feeling she wasn't going to stop talking until she got her way. She might look like a defenseless angel, but she wasn't. Not with that tongue.

Teddi searched his face for a sign. "Do we have a deal?"

"Okay, Missouri. We have a deal," he agreed. "I'll have the papers drawn up as soon as I get a chance."

"Where I come from, a handshake is good enough."
She offered him her hand.

He took it. Her fingers felt so delicate in his. "Well,
I've got to go."

She looked startled. "Where?"

"I work, remember? I'll be back at one. If Broadway hasn't snapped you up by then, I'll expect to meet
you downstairs at the store." To keep from kissing her,
he skimmed his forefinger down her upturned nose.
"See you, Missouri." The memory of her kiss last
night haunted him as he walked to the door.

"Where can I get a copy of *Variety*?" she asked,
calling after him.

"There's a newsstand on the next block," he told
her, his hand on the door. He saw the hesitant look
pass over her face. "What is it?"

"Could I borrow some money?"

He walked back in and pulled out his wallet. He put
ten dollars on the table in front of her. "In New York
less than a day, and in debt already," he teased.

"I'll pay you back," she promised.

"The tab is growing," he told her.

And then he was gone.

She sat at the table, listening to the early-morning
street noises and thinking about Keith. If he had
walked into her life a few years down the road, she
thought, she would have done everything in her power
to make him hers. He was by far the most appealing
man she had ever met. But the timing was wrong. All
wrong. She wasn't looking for a relationship; she
didn't have the time to devote to one. What she was

looking for was a break. And, she promised herself, come hell or high water, she was going to get it.

With that she rose. There was a brand-new day outside, and she was going to make the most of it.

Five

It took Teddi half an hour to find Keith's yellow pages. He kept his phone books in the kitchen, stacked neatly next to the pots in a cupboard by the stove.

The store below wasn't the only thing that could stand a little renovation, she thought as she scribbled down the address and phone number of the nearest bank that handled traveler's checks. His filing system was a little off, too.

The thought of working with Keith made her smile. "Theodora, you're losing sight of your goal," she told herself sternly, replacing the phone book. Teddi rose. She had promised herself that if she didn't land a job in six months, she would go back home, so it was definitely time to get started. Taking the money Keith had lent her, she walked out of the apartment.

The streets of New York were far less threatening in the daylight. Teddi's normally outgoing nature surfaced, and she walked cheerfully toward her destination, smiling at people as she went. Very few returned her smile, or even acknowledged her existence. She decided that was their problem, not hers. There was something to be said for growing up in a small town, she thought.

At nine in the morning the pedestrian traffic was brisk, the street traffic was heavy and the vendors at their freshest. She was amazed at the variety of things they had for sale. Just before she crossed one street an eager-looking teenager hooked her arm and tried to sell her an assortment of bracelets. She shook her head and walked on.

She saw someone across the street who looked like Keith. She hurried to catch up, but once she did, she discovered that she had made a mistake. She also discovered anticipation drumming through her veins. Odd, she mused. She hadn't reacted that way before, not to a man. A role, maybe, but not a man.

She couldn't get Keith out of her mind. What kind of a child had he been? she wondered. Had he indulged in games the way she had, or had he been a solemn child, following a cook around when he wasn't keeping to himself—and eating chocolate?

Catching sight of the street sign on the corner, she suddenly realized that she had overshot her destination by two blocks. She backtracked, telling herself that this was what she got for letting her mind wander.

Her business at the bank took the better part of two hours. The man behind the desk was brisk, efficient and just sympathetic enough to make her reevaluate her sentiments about New Yorkers. After filling out several forms and producing the list of her traveler's check numbers, she received a new checkbook. She slipped it inside her pocket and kept her hand protectively over it as she made her way home.

Walking up the avenue, she encountered more vendors: women selling flowers; young boys hawking trinkets. She absorbed it all, loving the vitality she found on the street.

She spent her first check on a purse to replace the one that had been stolen. It wasn't until she felt the familiar sensation of a strap over her shoulder that she felt whole again. After that it took her a few minutes to get her bearings. She blessed whoever had had the foresight to number the streets consecutively instead of giving them whimsical names. It made getting around so much easier.

Just before she reached the apartment she located the newsstand Keith had mentioned. Newspapers and magazines in Willow Grove were sold either in the local drugstore or from small coin-operated machines. She thought it a little odd that a human being would want to stand in a small, rectangular crate all day, framed by magazines and papers of all sizes, shapes and colors.

The man who sat in the midst of all this wore a cap on his head despite the heat and a loud shirt open at the throat. Tufts of springy white hair peered out. He looked like a wizened Buddha. The half-closed eyes were deceptive, however.

"Do something for you, lady?" he asked pointedly.

Teddi looked at him in surprise. He had appeared to be falling asleep. Taking a step back, she bumped into a man, who grunted something and continued walking. "Do you carry *Variety*?"

"A showgirl, eh?" He nodded knowingly.

She smiled at him. "I hope so."

He pushed his cap back, a frown puckering his features. "Take my advice, lady. Find yourself a nice fella and settle down. Showgirls don't last. They ruin their feet, and then who remembers them?" He waved a pudgy hand dismissively.

"Shirley MacLaine started out in the chorus," Teddi pointed out.

"Okay, one."

Teddi grinned. "And Ann Miller."

He shrugged, conceding the point. "Okay, maybe two."

She was getting warmed up. "So did Lucille Ball."

That impressed him. She could see the round face open up. "Are you funny?"

"Not intentionally," she had to admit.

The lids drooped again. "Like I said, find yourself a fella."

She leaned forward, amusement lighting her features. "While I'm looking for this 'fella,' can I read a copy of *Variety*?" That made two strangers she had met who had been kind in their own way. Not to mention Keith. New York wasn't such a cold place after all.

The man scratched the back of his head, pushing his cap over his eyes. "There was a copy around here someplace." Heavy hands shuffled magazines around from place to place. "Ah, here we go." He held it up. "Last copy."

"For luck," Teddi said. She pulled out the money Keith had given her. The man shoved the fat paper at her with one hand as he made change with the other. She pocketed it absently as she began to walk away.

"Good luck," he called out.

She turned and waved at him, then began to leaf through the paper anxiously. Any casting news would be here. The street, its color, the people around her, all ceased to exist. She might as well have been alone on a desert island.

Keeping one eye on where she was going, she scanned the paper with the other. By the time she had reached the street door, she had gone through half the paper with no results. After letting herself in she hurried up the narrow stairs and opened the door to her apartment. Spreading out the paper on the floor, she sat down cross-legged and went on reading. And hoping.

Finally she found a small ad calling for dancers to audition for an off-off-Broadway play on Friday. Today was Monday, she thought. That gave her four days to get into top condition—and pray.

She hurried to change into her leotard.

Keith was getting progressively more restless as the day wore on. He was walled in by cars as far as the eye could see. The city was definitely overcrowded, he thought irritably. The exhaust from the bus in front of him filled his empty cab. He muttered an oath and jockeyed for position in the next lane.

Usually he enjoyed driving. Even in the cutthroat arena of Manhattan, where reflexes needed to be honed to a fine edge, the constant weaving in and out and the need to be alert only served to sharpen his mind. He enjoyed working with his senses wide open.

But not today. Today was different. He had already missed three fares, beaten out by other drivers who were quicker in responding to hands held aloft and piercing whistles. Now he stopped at a red light.

It was her fault.

All morning she had kept on intruding into his consciousness at the most inopportune times.

Several horns blasted at once, and Keith realized that the light had turned green. Muttering under his breath, he moved his foot off the brake and onto the gas pedal.

He had been a fool to let her talk him into renting the apartment to her. The smart thing would have been to rent the apartment, all right, but to someone else. Someone who could pay him the going rate. He knew the place wasn't much, but "not much" in Manhattan was getting a king's ransom these days. Granted, it wasn't in the heart of the city, but it was close enough to count. And the bus stopped right on the corner.

A smile formed on his face. That was what he had liked about the location of the store. All those buses stopping at his corner. All those passengers standing around, waiting, while the sight of chocolate tempted them from his store window. It would be a start. A damn good one.

That was what he was supposed to be thinking about, he told himself. His start. His chocolate. Not some dewy-eyed dynamo who had long legs, blond hair that swirled around like a wayward cloud and a mouth that begged to be kissed. And a nightgown that didn't hide very much.

He slammed on his brakes as a cab cut in front of him, scooping up the fare who had been on the corner. He hadn't even seen the guy. He sighed, massaging the cramp in his neck. It was going to be another hot one, he thought. The air was already stifling. He turned down the next block and tried his luck there.

Stay alert, Calloway, he ordered.

With any effort on his part, he would have outmaneuvered her, glib tongue or not. He wasn't one to be snowed under. Not unless he *wanted* it to happen. There it was, he admitted to himself. He had let her talk him into the lease because he didn't want her walking out of his life. Not yet. He wanted to get to know her. The admission surprised him. He had always been determined, single-minded, stubborn when

he wanted to be. He had never let his emotions rule
him. The closest he had ever come to showing emotion was as a child, when he had brought home those
strays. It had been empathy he felt for them at the
time. They were homeless, and he used to feel that way
himself, at least figuratively. His heart had gone out
to them.

But this was a different matter. He was attracted to
the sloe-eyed would-be dancer, attracted to her vitality, to her dauntless approach to life. To her. Period.

At some other time and in some other place that
would have been fine, but not now. Now he needed to
concentrate all his energy on making a go of his
dream. He didn't need someone like her around. Attachments caused complications, and he had enough
of those with what he was doing.

He knew that small businesses had a high mortality
rate within the first year. He knew the figures cold, in
fact, but that hadn't stopped him. It had only served
to goad him on.

"You have to go, Missouri. There's no place for you
in my life right now." He was going to have to tell her
that as soon as he saw her this afternoon. Besides, he
argued, they had totally different temperaments. He
saw things clearly, calculated the risks before he went
ahead with something. She sailed into things, eyes
closed, hopeful. No, a relationship between the two of
them would never work, no matter what the timing.

A woman dragging a very reluctant child waved at
him. He swerved, coming to a halt. She yanked the
child along in her wake and approached the cab. Keith

reached over and swung open the door. She gave Keith an address on Lexington Avenue as she stepped inside, and he pushed down the flag on the meter.

Who was he kidding? he thought as he headed back into traffic. Teddi didn't want a place in his life. She wanted a place on Broadway. She would be gone before he knew it. Most likely, she would take off just like the previous tenants: in the dead of night. Owing him money.

The thought of her departure didn't bring the smile he would have expected to his lips. He blamed it on the heat. Everyone was contrary during a heat wave.

As if echoing his thought, the child kicked the back of Keith's seat.

"He's a little irritable today," the woman apologized, embarrassed.

"Aren't we all," Keith muttered, forcing his mind back on the road.

He brought the cab in with a very small tab for his day's work. The dispatch officer frowned at him and asked him if he had been sleeping at the wheel. Keith gave him a cool smile and said that it was so hot, everyone had decided to stay indoors. He was in no mood for a confrontation with the man. It seemed that everyone had become nasty-tempered in the heat wave. But, then, A. J. Weiss had never been exactly jovial to begin with.

Impulsively Keith stopped at Sal's on his way home. Despite the heat the place was packed. It was the tail end of the lunch hour, and though Sal had never gotten around to installing an air conditioner, his customers were loyal

"Beats me how you don't melt away into nothing," Keith told his friend when he reached the counter.

The tall, painfully thin man turned around, his ever-present grin fixed on his face, but all he said was "So, what'll it be?"

"A pizza with everything."

The dark eyes widened knowingly. "Going to see that pretty lady I saw you with last night?"

Keith looked away from the man's direct gaze, his eyes fixed on the floor. "She's, um, staying in the other apartment."

"Hey, hey!" Sal clapped him on the back, grinning. "You lucky dog. Wait." He held up a hand. "I've got one coming out of the oven in a minute. Hey, Angelo, wait on these nice people, okay?" he called to his son, gesturing toward the other customers at the counter. He beckoned for Keith to step over to the side.

"She got a sister?"

"It's nothing like that," Keith protested. "To tell you the truth, I saved her from a mugging last night."

In Sal's opinion, the story was obviously getting better and better. His dark eyes shone. "I bet she was grateful."

"Sal, I've only got my mind on business."

Sal shook his head, the damp black curls sticking to his temples. "My friend, I've always told you, all work and no play is very, very boring. Also not healthy." He opened the top oven. A blast of heat hit them both as he pulled out one of his masterpieces.

"If I want health," Keith told him as Sal packaged the creation, "I'll eat your pizza."

Sal grinned. "Here. Enjoy!"

Keith grinned, picking up the large flat box gingerly. "I will."

"More than the pizza," Sal called out after him.

Keith walked quickly to his apartment, telling himself that he was hurrying because he was hungry. He refused to admit that he was moving quickly to see if she was waiting for him.

"Maybe she found someplace to audition," he said under his breath. If that was the case, he was sure she wouldn't even give her promise to help out a second thought.

"And then you'll have an entire hot pizza on your hands." He suddenly remembered that last night's pizza hadn't been finished. "And half a cold one in the refrigerator."

He called himself a fool.

He called himself a bigger fool when his heart gave a lurch in his chest when he saw her standing out on the street. She was holding flowers in her hand.

He moved gracefully, she thought. Like an athlete. He must exercise, or he wouldn't have that kind of build. Biceps didn't just happen, she told herself, remembering what he had looked like in the hall last night. Biceps took effort. A lot of effort. She twirled the bouquet of carnations in her hand, twisting the green wrapper nervously.

This was the second time she had reacted nervously at the sight of him. What was it about the man that did that to her? And why did it have to be happening now, of all times? Why not later, after her career had been established?

"What are you doing down here?" he asked. God, he was glad to see her. His hands tightened on the box to keep from touching her face, and he found himself annoyed at the strength of his reaction.

"I was afraid I'd miss you and you'd start working without me." She put the bouquet on top of the box. "I don't welsh on my promises."

"Nice to know." He nodded at the flowers. "What's this?"

"Flowers."

"I can see that. Who gave them to you?"

"Nobody. I bought them for you."

Her answer left him speechless for a moment. "No one's ever given me flowers before."

She smiled. "Then I'm the first."

The first, he thought, for a lot of things. It had him worried. *She* had him worried. He cleared his throat. "No luck with the auditions?"

"There aren't any until the end of the week. I'm all yours until then."

She said it so innocently that he had to struggle to keep the grin from his face. The teasing, flippant retort he would have liked to make died a silent death.

Teddi wondered why he was looking at her so strangely. Other men had stared at her openly. Quite a few, actually. She was used to that. But there was something more in Keith's face, something she couldn't quite identify. "You brought food," she said, eyeing the box.

He had almost forgotten what he was holding. "I forgot we had some left over. Are you getting sick of pizza?"

"Never," she said with delight.

He followed her up the stairs, watching the way her hips moved as she walked. She was wearing a pair of very short shorts. He had never seen a more perfect pair of legs.

He was very grateful that his hands were otherwise occupied.

Six

___

What kind of a person would buy a rubber chicken?"
Teddi asked, holding one up by the legs. It dangled
from her fingers, a ridiculous testimony to the previous tenants' failure as businessmen.

"I don't know, but it's obvious that not too many
of them showed up at the store." Keith cleared a spot
on the cluttered counter, braced his hands on either
side and jumped up. He watched her as she moved
around the crowded store, the one ray of sunshine in
the dreary place. "I was going to wait out their lease
when I moved in here, but they left a month before it
was up—owing three months' rent."

Small wonder, she thought. Teddi turned slowly
around. Lemon-yellow wallpaper covered two walls of

the store. It was so bright that it almost hurt her eyes. Items as ridiculous as those she had found in her apartment last night were displayed everywhere she looked.

She dropped the rubber chicken into a box. And so starts the cleaning, she thought. "Are you going to turn this into a big kitchen?" She gestured around the room.

Did she know just how good she looked in that simple outfit of hers? Keith wondered as he watched her. No, it wasn't the white shorts and light green tank top. Any one of a number of attractive women could have worn that combination and he would have given them no more than a glance. What was it about her that kept her lingering in his mind, nudging aside all his other thoughts? She was like a fever in his blood, yet she hadn't tried to be anything but what she was.

Maybe that was the trouble.

Teddi looked at him expectantly. Why didn't he answer her? Why was he looking at her like that, as if he were trying to find a niche to file her in? "Keith?" she prodded when he still didn't say anything.

Abruptly he remembered her question. "No, I'm going to convert it into a shop, with the kitchen in the back."

"The back. There's more?" She said the words with dread. More rooms meant more cleaning. She wandered over to the sickly mauve curtain in the rear of the shop. Keith slid off the counter and followed her. She slowly slid the curtain along its track and discovered a room not much larger than a walk-in closet. It was filled to overflowing with more unsold stock.

"First," he said slowly, aware of how neatly their bodies seemed to fit together in the crammed area, "I have to build a back. I figure I can tear down the back wall and add another hundred square feet. Just enough to house my equipment and give me a little room to work."

She had grown up around men who were handy with tools. They *had* to be. But Keith had grown up with servants. She couldn't picture him with a hammer in his hand. "Do you know how?"

"I know a little about carpentry. I spent a summer helping a friend fix up his beach house once." What would the curve of her neck feel like beneath his fingers? he wondered. Beneath his lips? "Near Martha's Vineyard." His hands were on her shoulders before he could stop himself. "Besides," he continued slowly, "I've contracted out some of the work to a plumber and an electrician."

The odd flutter she had felt in her stomach when she watched him approach earlier returned, but now it had grown into a wave. She let him turn her around, knowing that her body would brush against his. Anticipation tingled along her spine.

He'd never seen eyes so blue, so innocent, or a mouth that was so desirable.

Teddi searched for something to say. She, who was never at a loss for words, could think only, He's going to kiss me again.

She felt her anticipation growing to exhilaration at the thought, and yet she was anxious at the same time. Getting involved with him had been the furthest thing from her mind when she had decided to move in. This could develop into an awkward situation if things didn't work out. He was just across the hall, and her landlord to boot. She had promised herself no entanglements, no complications, until she got settled and felt secure about her future. And here she was, getting tangled. Her eyes closed as his mouth met hers.

He hadn't been mistaken. Her lips were sweet, the kind that made a man want to come back again and again for more. He pressed her against him, his hands gliding along the smooth expanse of her delicate back. He calmed an urge to slip his hands beneath her blouse and explore her tender skin. He felt her breasts strain against his chest, and a liquid fire exploded within him. If he wasn't careful, things could get out of hand. He couldn't let that happen. He had work to do. Within two months there was going to be an important chocolate manufacturers' convention held in Dallas, and he had to be ready for it. Every moment was precious to him.

As was her kiss. For that very reason he gently pushed her away.

Teddi blinked, her mind a muddle of sensations. This was worse than last night. And better. Her body demanded more, reaching for something that lay behind a door she hadn't opened yet. It took her a moment to steady her breathing.

"We'd better get to work," Keith said, letting her go and turning away.

She nodded, grateful that things had stopped where they had, and very, very confused.

For the next three days they stayed outside each other's reach. By silent agreement, they felt safer that way. As if to help shore up their defenses, they painstakingly stated just how much their respective fledgling careers meant to them. Neither one would admit it, but they both thought the so-called truth rang just a little hollow.

Teddi, Keith discovered, was a tireless worker. He didn't know how she kept herself busy during the morning, when he worked, but when he returned to the store she was right there beside him. She scraped wallpaper, swept an unbelievably neglected floor and boxed gag gifts that ran the gamut from mildly amusing to positively kinky. She also learned an incredible amount of information about chocolate.

"You're kidding," she insisted one afternoon, putting down the piece of chocolate he had given her and eyeing it suspiciously.

Keith rocked back on his heels, taking a respite from laying the new floor. He looked at her expression and laughed. "No, that's what they believed. Mixed with water, maize and spices, the Indians believed that ground cocoa beans were an aphrodisiac. Of course, only the aristocracy was allowed to have any." He surveyed his work. The bright cream-colored linoleum shot through with threads of gold was a definite improvement over what had been there before. He rose and wiped his hands on the back of his jeans. "The Aztecs believed that chocolate was brought down from the Garden of Life by Quetzalcóatl."

She wasn't sure if he had said a name or coughed. She brushed her bangs out of her face, her scraper poised. "Who?"

"Their god. According to legend, he gave them chocolate as a consolation for having to live on Earth."

"I know a lot of people who'd probably be willing to believe that one." She frowned as she let the scraper drop to her side. Something he had said earlier popped into her mind. "But with—how much did you say was imported?"

"Four hundred and sixty million pounds," he tossed off. He leaned against the wall. There was only a little more of the floor to lay. He could do it tomorrow.

She shook her head at the figure. "With all that cocoa coming in each year, being turned into chocolate, how can you possibly think you'll be able to make a go of it?"

He came up behind her. She was on her knees after having wrestled with a stubborn section of wallpaper for the better part of an hour. Feeling at a disadvantage, she struggled to her feet.

Keith took her hand and helped her. "Do you know how many beautiful young women come to New York each year to make it on the Broadway stage? How many travel out to Hollywood to turn the town on its ear?"

Back to the familiar argument, she thought. "I don't want to turn it on its ear," she protested. "I just want to make a living."

"Same here."

The defensiveness that had risen so quickly dissipated just as fast. Teddi grinned. "I guess we both have our work cut out for us."

"Something like that." Reluctantly he let go of her hand. "You believe that you'll make a difference, and I believe my cocoa beans will."

"You're growing your own?" She flopped down on one of the two chairs that Keith had brought in. She couldn't remember when she had felt this exhausted.

He joined her, straddling the other chair. He leaned his head on his crossed hands. "No, the cacao tree requires a lot of love and care. It's sensitive and temperamental, like a woman." The smile in his eyes belied his serious expression. At his comment Teddi tossed her head, her ponytail brushing against her bare back. "Besides, it doesn't even bear fruit for four years. No, it's just that I'm getting my beans from a different source. Most of the beans now come in from the Ivory Coast, Brazil and Ghana. An investor, someone my father knows, told me I could get some exceptional beans from the Caribbean."

Teddi sighed, her eyes closed. "I wish I were in the Caribbean."

Her dark lashes barely touched her cheekbones, which were flushed from the heat and from exhaustion. She made quite a picture, he thought. "Tired?" he asked sympathetically. They had been at it for six hours. On the radio an oldies station was playing a loud, lively tune that contrasted sharply with how they felt.

Teddi nodded wearily. "My arms have gone numb. Am I still holding the scraper?"

"No," he said, laughing. He rose and stood in front of her. "I feel guilty working you so hard." He took her arm and began to massage it.

"That's okay. I'm a dancer. I'm used to slave drivers... Oh, that feels good," she murmured.

"Here, let me have the other one." He took it and began to knead her forearms.

She raised her eyes hopefully. "You know, my back really aches."

Keith went behind her chair and placed his hands on her shoulders. They felt so frail. He looked down at his hands, spread out on either side of her neck. They could easily span her waist, he judged. He began massaging. "Too hard?"

"Mmm." She sounded as if she were in ecstasy. "Wonderful, just wonderful."

He would have liked to hear her sound like that with her supple body beneath his. An image flashed through his mind. He was making love to her out in the open, someplace where flowers could rival her sweet scent. It was filling his senses now, clouding his mind and making him want her with a fierceness he had never felt before.

Teddi could feel his fingers tighten on her shoulders. His smoldering desire seemed to transmit itself through his hands and into her. She straightened slightly. A tingling sensation began in her breasts, and a warm, lazy feeling flowed through her thighs.

"What do you say to dinner?" As if suddenly aware of what he was doing, Keith withdrew his hands.

She felt a sharp, overwhelming emptiness. For a moment she couldn't cope with his rejection. What rejection? Her feelings were totally out of proportion for what had transpired. Something was wrong, or was she just experiencing something different, something she had never experienced before? she wondered, at a loss to understand what was happening to her. "I say yes."

"I kind of suspected that." They tried to ignore the intense feelings they had just experienced. There was a sense of uneasiness in their banter, as if they were lying to themselves and they knew it. "What's your pleasure?"

She stood and looked up at him with soulful eyes— she barely came up to his chin. She fought an incredible urge to say, "You," and answered, instead, "Food."

He took her chin into his hand. "Want to narrow it down a little?"

"Surprise me."

He wanted to. For a moment he wanted to surrender to the passion drumming at the corners of his soul, demanding that he stop being so logical, that he stop thinking at all and just do what he had wanted to since he had first seen her. With difficulty, the practicality that had seen him through all his life struggled to the surface and he put aside his needs.

"How does Chinese food sound?"

"It sounds terrific. Just give me time to change out of these grimy clothes."

He looked down at his own sweat-soaked T-shirt. "That makes two of us. The restaurant is casual, but I don't think they'd welcome someone with tar all over them." In an unguarded moment, he took her arm. It was a tender gesture, a gesture that showed he cared. In its simplicity, it exposed his feelings.

Teddi was quick to realize that her own feelings made her nervous. She blurted out, "That's okay," as she moved ahead of him. "I can still walk under my own power." Even if you *are* turning my knees to water, she added silently.

Her flippant remark stung, but he was careful not to change his expression. "Don't use up all the hot water," he called after her as she ran up the stairs.

"Hot?" She turned to look at him from the top of the stairs. She lifted her hair off her neck and fanned it with her free hand. "The last thing in the world I want is a hot shower."

He decided that a cold shower might be just what he needed himself. That, and to hold on to his priorities.

"I just might stay here all night," Teddi sighed as she leaned back against the padded seat in the booth. The waiter had already come and gone with their cocktails and she was now facing, quite happily, the main course. "God bless whoever invented air conditioning."

That reminded him. "I'm having the building wired for air conditioning."

Her fork hovered over the sweet-and-sour pork. "I think I'm in love."

He raised his brow. "Is that all it takes to win your love? Air conditioning?"

She absorbed every detail, every nuance, of the handsome man in front of her. His slightly square jaw. The deep blue eyes, the way his chestnut hair curled about his temples and brushed against his collar. Coupled with someone like you, she thought in answer to his question. But aloud she said, "Right now, it's a start."

The words, though spoken easily, held an undercurrent of something more. Teddi felt compelled to clarify her position. "Actually, when the time comes, I'd like to fall in love with someone who'd worship the ground I walk on."

"Sounds reasonable."

"Someone who'd support me and know just how much my career means to me. Someone—" she looked directly at him, remembering his earlier comment "—who didn't think that theater people were all flaky."

"If you had known my ex-brother-in-law, Jim, you'd understand why I feel the way I do. He sat around waiting for someone to ask him to fill Olivier's shoes. Finally he just left for Hollywood, taking most of Emily's money with him. He said he'd send for her

once he got established. That was five years ago." He
paused for a second, thinking of his sister. She was a
chemist now. Their father was very proud of her—finally. "She's still waiting, even after the divorce papers arrived. My father got a lot of pleasure out of
saying, 'I told you so.'" He looked down into the cup
of tea he held between his fingertips. The hot amber
liquid swished along the sides. "Just the way he's
biding his time waiting to say that to me."

She looked at him sympathetically and touched his
hand. He looked up. In the dimly lit restaurant, she
looked even more virginal, even more sensuously appealing. She wore a simple pale yellow sundress cut
low in the front. It made his fingers itch to touch her
soft skin. "I had a wonderful father. A little old-
fashioned, maybe, but he was a rock anytime you had
a problem." She smiled ruefully as memories played
through her mind. "I supplied him with my share of
those."

Yes, he could see her creating problems. She certainly was for him. "How would he have felt about
what you're doing?"

She straightened slightly as she looked down at her
plate. "He would have disapproved. He was very
practical in his own way. He would have been there for
me if I failed—but he would have expected me to fail."
She raised her eyes. He saw her raw look of determination. "I'm not going to fail."

Somewhere in the past few days, between the torn
wallpaper, the dust and the army of gag gifts, he had
begun to care for her as a person in his life. He didn't

want to see her hurt. She seemed so blind to any negative possibilities. She was an eternal optimist.

"But if you do—" he began tentatively.

The waiter came with their fortune cookies and cleared away the dishes. Teddi didn't notice, seeing only the handsome, annoyingly practical man across from her. "I won't," she said firmly. "As long as I have a positive attitude, everything will be all right. I have faith in myself, even if no one else does. And tomorrow—" she broke open her cookie with a snap "—I'm going to get a part."

He had forgotten about the audition. Out of the blue, he felt threatened. By what, he wasn't sure. He told himself that he had no business lecturing her. A man who sank his entire fortune into chocolate couldn't be considered the voice of wisdom and practicality.

But it was all right for him, he thought. He had something to fall back on if he failed. On the other hand, what would she do if they said, "Don't call us— we'll call you?" It would shatter her. Or if they suggested trading a role on the stage for the proverbial roll in the hay? He began to feel angry.

He reminded himself that innocent-looking though she was, there was a strong core underneath. He remembered the look on her face that first night in the alley—outrage, not fear. She'd be all right.

In any event, she wasn't his concern. Or was she?

"Nervous about tomorrow?" he asked as he placed the bill on the waiter's silver plate. The man whisked it away before the money hit the tray.

SILHOUETTE DELIVERS FIRST-CLASS ROMANCE— DIRECT TO YOUR DOOR

Mail the Heart sticker on the postpaid order card today and you'll receive:

— **4 new Silhouette Desire novels—FREE**
— **an elegant pen & watch set—FREE**
— **and a surprise mystery bonus—FREE**

But that's not all. You'll also get:

Money-Saving Home Delivery

When you subscribe to Silhouette Desire, the excitement, romance and faraway adventures of these novels can be yours for previewing in the convenience of your own home at less than retail prices. Every month we'll deliver 6 new books right to your door. If you decide to keep them, they'll be yours for only $1.95 each. That's 30¢ less per book than what you pay in stores. And there is no extra charge for shipping and handling!

Free Monthly Newsletter

It's the indispensable insider's look at our most popular writers and their upcoming novels. Now you can have a behind-the-scenes look at the fascinating world of Silhouette! It's an added bonus you'll look forward to every month!

Special Extras—FREE

Because our home subscribers are our most valued readers, we'll be sending you additional free gifts from time to time as a token of our appreciation.

OPEN YOUR MAILBOX TO A WORLD OF LOVE AND ROMANCE EACH MONTH. JUST COMPLETE, DETACH AND MAIL YOUR FREE OFFER CARD TODAY!

Remember! To receive your free books, pen and watch set and mystery gift, return the postpaid card below. But don't delay!

DETACH AND MAIL CARD TODAY.

If offer card has been removed, write to: Silhouette Books, 120 Brighton Road, P.O. Box 5084, Clifton, NJ, 07015-9956

"I'm never nervous," she told him. And she wasn't, not really. Except for isolated moments around him. "Nerves just get in the way."

She sounded different from the woman who had been working side by side with him for four days. The light, innocent note was gone, replaced by confidence. She believed in herself. Just as he did in himself, he thought. And yet they were so different.

He slid out of the booth and waited for her to join him. "Where is the audition?"

"In a little theater in Greenwich Village. *Man of La Mancha* started in the Village, you know," she said brightly. They walked out of the restaurant.

She's counting on the same success hitting her, he realized. Protectively he put his arm around her shoulders, though her cool skin played havoc with him.

She liked the feeling of his arm around her, of having him around. Can two people get used to each other in so short a time? She knew a lot about his dream, his background, his chocolate, she thought with a wry smile, but what about *him*?

That will have to wait, for now, Teddi. You've got auditions to attend, worlds to conquer. And so does he.

The streets were empty in comparison to how they had been just a few hours ago. Stars vied with the tops of skyscrapers for position in the heavens. The evening felt comfortable for the first time since she arrived in New York City. She felt comfortable.

Unconsciously she leaned against his arm, allowing herself to be guided back home. She marveled at how quickly the apartment had become that to her. You're making attachments, she warned herself. And attachments meant complications. She needed to focus on only one thing: her career.

She was reluctant to have the evening end and tried to think of an excuse to make him stay once they reached her door.

He seemed to be having the same problem, she realized. For a moment he stood silent, just looking at her. "I don't know if I made myself clear before, but I really do appreciate all your help with the store."

"Then can you give me a ride to the theater tomorrow?" she suggested.

There was no resisting her appeal. "What time?"

"They start at eight. I want to be there at seven."

"Ouch." He winced. "That early?"

"They'll all be waiting on line."

He nodded. "I'll get Nathan to give us a ride. He owes me." His hands slipped around her waist. They *could* span it, he confirmed.

"Well, um, I'd better... get... some... rest." Teddi's words came slowly as she watched the fire rise in his eyes.

"In a minute, Missouri, in a minute." His lips just touched hers and the control he prided himself on was wrenched from him. The hell with control, he thought, pulling her into his arms. If there was a price to pay, he'd pay later, not now. Now he wanted only to taste her sweet flavor mingling with his. Her parted lips were an invitation he couldn't resist.

When he heard her moan, something primitive came forth within him, something that wanted to possess her more than he wanted to maintain control, more than he wanted to breathe.

Teddi pressed her body against his. She raked her hands through his hair, loving the feel of it, loving the feel of him. Loving him.

The word exploded in her brain. Love? Oh, no, not now. She couldn't. She wouldn't.

She was.

Trembling, she looked up at him, wanting to tell him what she felt, wanting to share what had suddenly ignited within her. "Keith, I—"

"Have an early day tomorrow." His words were measured as he tried to steady his breathing. "You'd better turn in." Before I lose all control.

As she turned to open her door and walk in, she loved him even more for not pressing his advantage.

Keith stood there for a long time, staring at the closed door.

Seven

Jealousy was an emotion Keith had never dealt with before. Yet he felt its uncomfortable grip the following morning. Teddi's exuberance was overwhelming. There was a glow about her, a glow he wished he—not the audition—had inspired. It served to remind him that he was growing too attached to her. Dancing in the theater meant everything to her. She had said as much. Undoubtedly, once she found work and began making money, she'd leave. He'd be a fool to think otherwise.

"How do I look?" she asked, turning around for his inspection at her door. She was wearing a sea-green wraparound skirt over a matching leotard and tights.

Her hair was held back by two tortoiseshell combs, a blond river held in abeyance.

He was about to say beautiful, but he knew that wasn't what she wanted to hear. He shoved his hands deep in his pockets. "Capable. Very capable." She didn't seem to notice the lack of enthusiasm in his words.

She tossed her head, delighted. "Good. That's how I feel." She hoisted her purse strap onto her shoulder and glanced inside to make sure she had remembered her tap shoes. She surprised him by lacing her fingers through his in an act that was simultaneously a sign of friendship and of intimacy. Confident or not, she needed someone in her corner, however briefly. "Well, let's go."

She sat ramrod-straight in the back seat of Nathan's cab, looking neither left nor right. He knew she was psyching herself up. He leaned back, fascinated by this other side to her. Was the real Teddi the bubbly woman who cleaned at two in the morning, or this quiet professional? Or were they both part of a greater whole he didn't know yet?

They made no attempt at conversation. The air was filled nonetheless with the sound of a low, rumbling voice that went on and on for its own sake; Nathan hadn't stopped talking since he had picked them up.

Keith had met the tall, thin black man on his first day on the job. It was Nathan who had shown him the ropes. Nathan could also connive and persuade Keith to cover for him from time to time. Nathan worked nights and wasn't always up to completing his shift.

"An actress, huh?" Nathan chuckled. It was a well-meaning laugh, half sympathetic, half envious.

"Dancer," Teddi corrected.

"Sure do have the legs for it." He glanced over his shoulder, a warm, friendly look in his brown eyes. "If you don't mind my saying so."

Teddi shook her head, offering him a grateful smile; her ego could use a boost right about now.

Nathan turned back around. "Had a cousin who was a dancer. She wound up on the road a lot." And for the next thirty-three minutes, Teddi and Keith were treated to the adventures of his cousin, his aunt, his two brothers and a few relatives whose connection Teddi had missed.

She didn't let go of Keith's hand the whole time, and he felt her fingers tighten ever so slightly as they finally arrived at the theater. His sympathies went out to her, yet at the same time he told himself they shouldn't. She had chosen this route. He shifted in his seat. He was being unfair. Was this jealousy again?

Something small and haunting in her eyes called to him. If she didn't make it, now or at other auditions, she'd be crushed. If she did, he was afraid he'd soon see the last of her. He knew that all people in the arts weren't like his shiftless brother-in-law. But people who chose a life of such fierce competition had to be self-absorbed to a great extent. There wasn't room for much else, and what there was took second place, if even that. When the time came to become really involved with a woman, he couldn't accept second place.

Tied for first maybe, he thought wryly, but never second.

What was bothering him, he thought as he followed her out of the cab, was that he wasn't altogether sure he had that much of a choice in the matter anymore.

"God, look at them," Teddi said with a sigh, not moving from the curb. A human chain went clear to the end of the block and around the corner.

"A broken heart for every light on Broadway," Keith commented. He wanted to take her back home.

She gave him a reproachful side glance. "You certainly know the right thing to say."

He looked over her head at the people on line. "Just being realistic."

She fixed his crooked collar. "Don't be."

He kissed the palm of her hand. For a moment their eyes locked, unspoken messages passing between them.

Nathan leaned over in the car and craned his neck. "You coming on back?" he asked Keith. "I've got to report in."

To Teddi's surprise, Keith shook his head. He shoved his hands into his back pockets. "You go on. I'll grab another cab."

Nathan began to pull away from the curb.

"No." Teddi held up her hand. Nathan waited. "There's no need to hang around," she told Keith. She saw his concern, and it made her smile. "I'll be all right. Really. And you'll be late for work." Her smile lit up her eyes. "See? I can sound practical, too."

Why wasn't she nervous? he wondered. On line he could see hopefuls playing with their hair, pacing, fidgeting. Natural reactions. Yet she stood there, as peaceful as if she were going off to church. It bothered him. He was nervous for her, he realized. And for himself. He conceded. "Okay. I'd better go. Good luck." He bent to kiss her.

"Oh, no." She touched his lips, stopping him. "You're supposed to say 'break a leg.'"

He shrugged and then kissed her cheek. "Break a leg, if that's what you want."

"It is."

He got into the front seat next to Nathan. He turned to look at her, but she was already working her way up the block to secure her place in line.

"That's some foxy lady," Nathan commented, turning the cab around. "Yours?"

Keith turned and looked straight ahead, a stony expression on his face. "Nope."

"I see." Nathan merely grinned. "Ever tell you about the time my second cousin Jack fell in love with this lady juggler?"

"No." Keith sighed, resigned. "But I have a feeling you will."

Keith let Nathan drone on.

There was no warmth within the theater. It was ninety degrees, yet she felt cold. Even though some of the dancers near her smiled nervously at her or one another and some even exchanged vague words, everyone was wrapped up in an isolated, tense world where survival hung in the balance and outdoing one another was crucial.

It wasn't something she was used to.

Devoid of scenery, the stage was stark and only reinforced the feeling of alienation, of depressing isolation, that permeated the air. It mingled with the smells of perspiration and humidity. Excitement, despair, anticipation and fear echoed from all four corners as the dancers came and went, trying to meet the choreographer's demands. She wasn't sure she liked any of it. But she knew she had to be here, had to be part of it, had to dance.

Since she was five years old and an indulgent aunt had bought her first tap shoes and financed a year's worth of lessons, Teddi knew that this was what she wanted to do. She had said it anytime someone asked her what she wanted to be. When she was still young, it had been a source of smiles and labeled "cute." As she grew older, it had become a source of concern for her family. But she had remained steadfast.

And it was going to take more than one thin, sharp-faced choreographer to make her turn back on a lifetime of dreams.

"Next six!" the choreographer bellowed, annoyance dripping from his words. With arrogant superiority he turned to the man at his side. "Why are all the good people always taken?" His question was loud enough for everyone to hear. It was meant to cow the next batch of dancers.

Teddi took a deep breath and stood ready. She was sixth in line. The other women were all about the same age but varied in height and amount of experience. She tried not to think about the fact that she was a novice.

The choreographer, Anthony Andretti, looked them over. "All right, my lovelies, let's see if at least one of you doesn't move like a cow."

He went over the short routine and then stepped back. The music began again.

Teddi gave it everything she had. The clatter of taps filled the air. The others were good, she thought as she danced. So had the previous six been. She had watched them from the wings. But all Andretti had done was frown when they were through.

He duplicated that response when the music stopped. "Thank you, thank you. Leave your name and a place you can be reached with the girl at the door." He waved them off. His expression altered slightly as he watched them move offstage. "Hey, you—Blondie."

Teddi stopped, her heart hammering. Her eyes opened wide.

He beckoned impatiently. "Yes, I mean you."

Was he going to tell her she had made it? she thought, her head suddenly pounding with hope. He hadn't called anyone else over.

"Is this your first time?"

Her heart sank. "Yes."

He smirked. "It shows."

And then he turned his back on her to confer with his assistant.

It's not going to bother me, she told herself, feeling numb as she walked slowly off the stage. The man has the manners of a pig and probably the talent to go with it. If he didn't, he wouldn't be here. He'd be working on something important.

She told herself that her eyes were smarting from the pollution.

"Don't listen to him."

Teddi looked around and saw a statuesque brunette behind her. She was getting ready to go onstage. "You looked just great from where I was standing."

Teddi smiled in gratitude. "Thanks."

"Don't mention it." The woman turned to take her turn onstage. It was finally Teddi's turn with the woman at the stage door. Mechanically she recited her name and Keith's number, then walked out. For a moment, she stood outside the theater, her eyes adjusting to the daylight. It was over. Her first audition was over. She had waited in line for the better part of the morning, only to be insulted. For the first time in a long time, Teddi felt lonely.

"Need a cab, lady?"

She recognized the voice before she even turned around. She felt her smile forming, traveling up to her eyes and down to the tips of her fingers, taking over every part of her.

Keith stood, leaning against the hood of his car. The Off Duty sign was on.

"Oh, Keith." Without thinking, she threw her arms around him. She hadn't realized until this moment just how much it meant to her to have him there.

"Hey." Gently he put his arms around her. "Was it that bad?"

"It was awful," she moaned, resting her cheek against his chest.

He longed to kiss her, to stroke her head. The fragrance of her hair filled his senses. He just kept holding her. "You didn't make it?"

"It doesn't seem so."

Her voice was tired. He searched for words of comfort. "From what I gather, they don't usually make their decisions right on the spot. Maybe you'll get called back." He let her go.

"He said I danced like a rookie."

"Maybe you won't get called back," he agreed, opening the car door for her. She slid in. "But there'll be other shows." He eyed her carefully, waiting to see her reaction.

Teddi straightened her skirt, then twisted in her seat to look at him as he took the driver's side. "I know. But rejection hurts."

The engine came to life. "I know."

She pouted slightly. "When have you ever been rejected?"

"Never." He looked at her face and wanted to kiss the pout away. He turned the wheel and the cab joined the flow of traffic. "But I can empathize."

"It's not the same thing." She slouched in her seat, feeling dejected.

"Would you like to go to lunch, or would you rather wallow in self-pity?"

She studied his profile for a moment. She liked the fact that his nose wasn't perfect; it was a little on the Roman side, which gave his face character. "Both. How long before we reach the restaurant?"

"By the looks of this traffic, about another twenty-five minutes."

"Good. That'll be just about as long as I need to wallow."

He grinned. She was going to be all right.

"Hey." She suddenly sat up straight.

He thought there was something on the road, and his foot was hovering over the brake in an instant. "What's the matter?"

"Isn't today the day your equipment arrives?"

His foot returned to the gas pedal. How could he have forgotten that? Thoughts of Teddi and her audition had driven everything else from his mind. In only a few days, despite all his good intentions, she had succeeded in turning his well-ordered life upside down. "You're right."

"Cancel lunch," she murmured, resigned.

His mind began to race. The delivery truck would be there between one and five. "I'll get you back to the shop and get the cab back to the station. There's some ham in my refrigerator. Make yourself a sandwich, but keep your eye peeled for the delivery truck."

"A ham sandwich's poor consolation for a bruised ego," she sniffed.

"We'll see what we can do for your bruised ego later." He reached over and gave her hair a little tug.

* * *

"What's this all about?" Teddi asked.

She was standing in the doorway of what was to be his kitchen. Large pieces of machinery lined the wall, still under wraps. She had expected him to be busy making sure everything worked. Instead he was hovering around the table in the center of the room.

She had just come in to tell him that he was out of paint. Behind her a freshly painted pale beige wall dried. She watched him move about.

Keith had covered the table with a linen tablecloth and was now in the process of lighting two tall candlesticks that he had planted in silver holders. The lights gleamed on the two plates that framed them.

"Your consolation prize." Keith blew out the match.

"Let me guess. You're lighting candles and turning out the lights so that I don't see that dinner is going to be another round of ham sandwiches."

"Guess again." He produced two goblets and a bottle of red wine.

She looked at him uncertainly. "Are we celebrating something?" Had the choreographer called after all?

"Friday."

"Oh." He wasn't making any sense.

He crossed the room to her. "And—" he took the roller out of her hand "—the fact that you've been the best helper I've ever had." He ushered her to the table.

Keith pulled the chair out for her. "I'm the only helper you've had."

"Don't spoil it." He took a covered casserole from the wicker basket on the floor. "Sal sent this."

She eyed the dish. "Did he run out of boxes for the pizza?"

"His mother makes a mean lasagna."

"Lasagna?" Her taste buds were awakened. "Stop talking and let's eat."

He laughed as he took a metal spatula from the basket. "I had a feeling you'd say that." He uncovered the container and dished out a portion for her. "Wine?"

"I'd love it." She watched as he filled her glass. "What shall we drink to?"

"How about thirst?"

As he watched her press her lips together, thinking, he felt another wave of desire rising. All afternoon he had wrestled with it. He had watched her work hard, as she attempted to forget her disappointment, to blot out her introduction to the hard realities of the performing arts. He had ached to comfort her, to take her back into his arms and hold her. But he had restrained himself, knowing that this time there would be no holding back.

"How about success?" she suggested.

"In general?" He raised his glass to hers.

She shook her head. "Specifically. Ours."

At this point, he wasn't so sure that her success would be his. But he obliged her. Their glasses clinked.

Teddi found a toast for every glass of wine they shared as they finished and appreciated Mrs. Petruzillo's lasagna. They neatly split the bottle between them.

"You know," Teddi began slowly, the wine freeing her pent-up feelings. Clear-headed, she wouldn't have had the courage to admit this to him. "I was awfully glad to see you there this afternoon." Dark lashes framed her cornflower-blue irises as she smiled. "You're really very sweet."

"It comes from working with chocolate." He couldn't look at her. Not if he wanted to remain in control.

"Would you do something else for me?"

Her soft voice made him look up with anticipation. "What?"

"I need a hug."

"What?"

"A hug. A big, enveloping, world-blotting-out hug."

She didn't know what she was asking of him. "Missouri, I don't—"

"Please?"

He could have held himself in check, fought back his own feelings. But he couldn't fight hers, as well. Knowing he was going to be sorry, he stood. She rose at the same time. "You've got paint on your cheek." He wiped it off. Her cheek felt like silk. He ceased to wipe and began to caress.

"Where's my hug?" she murmured. His arms went around her. It felt so good, so right. "You know," she told him as his lips grazed the top of her head, "I don't have the time to fall in love."

"Me, neither." He couldn't stop himself. His lips trailed to her cheek, the one he had wiped the paint from.

"I've got a career to build."

"Same here." Kisses feathered to her other cheek.

"So what are we doing?" She arched her neck, inviting his lips to touch her throat. When they did, she moaned softly.

He felt his pulse rise as he touched his mouth to hers. "Beats the heck out of me."

The kiss was meant to be gentle, but as soon as his lips touched hers, it was fire touching fire. She kissed like a woman with needs and wants that matched his own. "I want you, Missouri."

Her body was hot against his. She slid her hands beneath his shirt. His abdominal muscles grew taut under her touch. "I know."

"You'll be sorry in the morning," he warned her. Was it the wine that spurred her? And why couldn't he summon the strength to resist?

"Maybe." She took his face between her hands and kissed his mouth hard. Tongue explored tongue, tasting wondrous things that went beyond description.

With his last ounce of control, he pulled his head away. "Turn back?" he offered. He wouldn't know how to deal with the ache inside if she did, but he knew he had to give her this final chance.

Teddi shook her head, her eyes clouded with need. "Not on your life."

He wasn't sure of himself, she realized. Since that first night when he had come to her rescue, she had thought of him as always being sure, as always being secure in all his actions. A humming filled her head. Maybe he was as afraid of this as she was. Maybe it was just as new to him, just as unexplored.

She was attaching too much romance to it, she thought as her arms entwined about his neck. He probably had had scores of women. But she had never had a man. No one had ever made her want to. Not until now. She offered him her lips.

He crushed her mouth to his. Her hair gleamed in the candlelight as he held her. His eyes closed and his other senses took control. He felt her heart beating against his chest. He was powerless to stop what was happening and ceased trying to. All he could do was hold himself back enough not to take her with the fierce passion that was drumming in his ears.

"My hands are callused," he said in apology even as he captured the soft, supple swell of her breast.

Teddi sucked in her breath as skin met skin. "It's all right," she whispered, feeling both drugged and aflame. "Everything's all right."

She thought it strange that she should assure him. She was the novice here. A sigh escaped her lips as he pulled off her top. He bent his head, kissing one breast and then the other. Blazing arrows shot through her. She tangled her fingers in his hair and felt herself being lifted. Her eyes opened, questioning.

"Not here," he told her.

She snuggled her head against his shoulder, trusting him. She put her arm around his shoulder, her fingers dipping lightly along his back. A ripple of muscle met her touch. Power. It served to heighten her excitement.

His lips touched hers again, and then he deepened the kiss as he made his way up the stairs. He stopped kissing her only long enough to take his key out of his pocket and open the door.

"Just like Scarlett O'Hara," she murmured.

He didn't answer, stunned at what was happening. His mouth moved over her throat and shoulders, breathing in her soft scent, before he finally lowered her to his bed. She lay there, a half-naked goddess with a pool of blond hair about her head. He didn't take his eyes off her as he stripped off his shirt. She raised her hands to him and he was beside her, his body heating from hers, his senses running wild. He wanted her all at once, now, yet wanted to prolong every blissful moment, preserving it for all eternity.

He had never wanted a woman this way, had never held himself in check like this. He knew that this was different, that she mattered the way none had before her and none would after her.

He caressed her with slow, mind-clouding strokes, taking her to plateaus and summits she had never reached before. He possessed her, leaving the imprint of his hand on every inch of her, claiming every part with restrained, deliberate passion.

Though his control was shaken, he kept his own needs at bay until hers rose to the same fever pitch. He drew apart the snap on her shorts and tugged them from her inch by agonizing inch. She raised her hips for him and he heard her moan.

Her needs sprang up in full force in every part of her body. Every area he didn't touch was jealous for his caress. She arched against his hand, wanting it to be everywhere at once. Closer. She needed him closer. Emotion built on emotion as her body demanded the highest plateau it could reach.

Open-mouthed kisses reduced her bones to liquid, frightening her even as she gloried in them. She loved the sensation of being nude beneath him, her taut body moving to the rhythm his created, to a music only they heard. She waited for the final moment, not knowing if she could bear any more pleasure. But still he kissed, still he stroked, his hand taking intimate possession of her.

When he entered, Teddi gasped, her fingers tightened on his shoulders. A shaft of guilt shot through Keith as he lifted his head. "Missouri, you're a virgin."

"Your virgin," she whispered softly.

He had no defenses left. Teddi became totally mindless, giving up her mind to a swirling sensation of colors and heat, tastes and delights, riding wave after cresting wave of passion until journey's end. Her arms tightened around him, trying to absorb everything about him, about what she felt.

Keith buried his face in the curve of her neck, loving her beyond anything.

Eight

Teddi opened her eyes. It hadn't been a dream. He was there, next to her. Sleeping. It was near morning. A crack of daylight poked through a separation in the curtains.

She lay still, her breath trapped within her lungs. Now what? What should she say? How should she act? Blasé? As if nothing had happened? Or should she allow that strange, wondrous feeling crowding every inch of her body to pour out?

She hadn't a clue. There was nothing in her past to draw on for a situation like this. For the morning after. A familiar nervous flutter filled her stomach. She couldn't blame the wine. The wine had only freed her, not made her do things against her will. She pulled the sheet up very slowly, not wanting to wake him.

This wasn't supposed to have happened. Not yet, not now.

Things don't always work out according to plan, she told herself. She had a feeling this wasn't exactly on Keith's agenda, either, not from what he had told her. The man has a business to tend to, she reminded herself. And she had a career to build. This should have happened later, much later, when things were settled, when she could concentrate on him.

Keith rolled over. His hair fell into his eyes. The sheet barely covered him. A warm feeling flashed through her. He opened his eyes. Instantly she became lost in them.

"Hi," she whispered.

He propped himself up on one elbow, then took a strand of her hair into his hand and sifted it through his fingers. In the early-morning light, it looked almost gold, not silver blond. "Hi, yourself."

He sounded serious. Teddi felt apprehensive.

Oh, God, is he regretting it? Is he wondering how to get me out of his bed?

She swallowed. Be direct; people respect honesty. She always had. Up to now. "What happens now?" she asked.

He stared down at her as he ran the back of his hand along her neck and collarbone. Teddi couldn't take her eyes from his face. "We have breakfast."

"Breakfast?" She repeated it as if it were a foreign word.

He nodded. "Yes, breakfast." Her scent began to fill his head. "Eventually."

"Eventually?"

A soft smile broke through. He ran his knuckles against her cheek. "Right now, there's an entirely different sort of hunger running through my veins." He knew he shouldn't perpetuate the situation, but his desire was stronger than his common sense. One taste of heaven was not enough. And this morning her eyes weren't lit with disappointment the way they had been last night, before they had made love. He only wanted to make sure that she hadn't made love with him because of the wine or because she had needed comforting after the audition. He needed to know that she made love with him because of *him*.

He buried his hands in her hair, drawing her face to his. Ever so lightly, his lips brushed against hers.

He opened the floodgates. The uncertainty, the nerves, the doubts, all fled. Later they might return, but right now the only thing she wanted in her mind, her body, her senses, was Keith. She slid her shoulders from the pillow, sinking further into the bed. He moved against her. The pressure was exquisite.

"I'm not getting you on the rebound, am I?"

She didn't understand. "Rebound?"

"Do you know—" he kissed the hollow of her throat and watched her pulse quiver there "—that you've echoed everything I've said in the past three minutes?"

"Echoed?" And then she laughed. A sense of ease returned. "Just what do you mean by rebound?" She saw a frown form on his face. She ran her fingers over his lips. The frown disappeared, and his lips parted to kiss each finger.

He could feel her stir beneath him, and it took everything he had to keep his mind on his thoughts. "Oh, that maybe you were trying to forget what happened in that dark theater."

After all the strutting, macho men she had encountered, Keith was a new experience. She traced the hard ridges of his chest. "If that was my object, I would have found an old movie to watch on TV." Her fingertips lightly grazed his nipple. She watched desire enter his eyes. "What happened last night happened too soon, out of order, but it didn't happen because you took advantage of a depressed, paint-streaked woman."

He brushed the bangs out of her eyes. "Nice to know."

"Are you going to kiss me?" she asked.

"Yes."

"When?"

"Right now."

"Good. I didn't want to make the first move again." She drew him closer.

Daylight grew insistent before they gave any thought to the outside world again.

Teddi rose from his bed, tugging at the corner of the sheet he was lying on. He watched her as she tucked it around her breasts. "Don't you think it's a little late for that?" Amusement lifted the corners of his mouth.

She raised her chin high, though her eyes sparkled with merriment. "My mother always said to maintain an air of mystery." With that, she strolled into his bathroom with all the dignity of a queen.

As he slipped on a pair of worn jeans, he heard her humming a show tune. She didn't need sheets around her to perpetuate an air of mystery, he thought. And he was totally mystified as to what was happening here. He had never veered from a plan, no matter how great the temptation. And he had never felt this way about a woman before. He couldn't find a name for it, or maybe the name that whispered itself to him was too frightening to accept just yet. The experience was, he thought as he raked his hand through his hair, definitely interesting.

He smiled to himself over his description. It was interesting, all right. The way capturing lightning in a bottle was interesting. But what happened once the storm was over? If he allowed himself to become involved now, would he be the same if she walked out of his life? She distracted him now. If he didn't get control of himself, she'd undermine everything he was doing, even if she didn't mean to. And once she was gone, he'd be left with nothing, not even his cherished dream. He couldn't *afford* to become involved.

Besides, he didn't want to come in second. And unless he missed his guess, one rejection wasn't about to deter her from trying to reach her goal. In her own way, she was as headstrong as he was. They were alike in the wrong way and different a lot of other ways. Think about it all later, he counseled himself.

"Are you fixing breakfast?" she called out.

"Can't you think of anything else but your stomach?" He made his way to the refrigerator and took out a carton of eggs.

"Sure—" her voice floated out "—but not when I'm hungry."

He took out four eggs and put the carton back. "How do you like your eggs?"

"On a plate."

He grinned. At least she wasn't fussy. No, she wasn't fussy, but she certainly was . . . something else. It was, he decided as he cracked the eggs into a bowl, like trying to hold mercury in the palm of your hand. If you tried to close your fist, it ran right through your grasp. The best way to enjoy it was to hold your palm steady and just watch it shimmer.

She came out of the bathroom, a towel wrapped around her upper torso.

"It doesn't go with your shorts," he commented as he nodded at them. Eggs met pan and sizzled.

"No," she agreed. "But my tube top seems to be mysteriously missing."

He remembered. "It's downstairs."

She nodded. "I'll go to my apartment and get something to put on."

"If you really feel you have to." He pretended to lunge for the towel. Teddi darted out of reach and ran all the way to her apartment.

Somewhere between breakfast and hooking up his equipment, he decided he was going to call Emily. It had been a while since he had spoken to his sister. They had never been close, especially as they grew older, but she might know someone who could help Missouri. He knew that during her short, tempestuous marriage, Emily had become acquainted with a good many actors. It was a shot in the dark, he realized as he connected the last hose to the device used for cleaning the cocoa beans. Missouri needed a break, and he wanted to help her. His generosity warred with the new sensation of jealousy. Life, he thought, had certainly gotten more complicated lately.

"What's that thing do?" Teddi asked as she walked into the kitchen. She looked at the machine from all angles. With all this machinery in the kitchen, there was hardly any space left to work, she thought.

"It blows the debris away from the beans. Sticks, stones, insects—you name it."

She tapped the gray metal. "Pay extra for that?"

He crouched low, trying to reach the electrical outlet. "The supplier sends them free."

"How about a demonstration?" She liked seeing him in his element. He seemed to be happiest when he was concentrating on making his dream a reality. Something had happened to her last night; she had reached out to him and he had been there for her. She was in love with him. There was no denying the fact. And she wanted to be part of everything he did, understand everything about him. She decided to start with his equipment.

"Later."

She felt slightly put off but managed to overcome the feeling. She pointed to another machine. "What's this one do?"

"It roasts the beans," he said without looking up.

"You could have saved your money. Just put the beans out on the sidewalk." She turned her head this way and that, attempting to release some of the tension she felt. Maybe she had gone too fast, dreamed too much. Men don't like feeling trapped, she reasoned. Maybe he's trying to sort things out, to understand his own feelings. Go slow. "And this one?"

He looked over his shoulder. "That separates the bean from the shell."

"All this for chocolate?"

"We haven't even gotten started yet." He got up. "That one grinds the beans." He gestured toward the corner. "And we haven't even gotten into mixing, rolling, kneading and whipping all the ingredients together."

"What kind of ingredients?" she asked innocently. The little chocolate angels in his cupboard sounded as if they were an awful lot of trouble.

"Ingredients to make my chocolate different from the others." It was an evasive answer and he knew it, but he couldn't help himself. He had guarded the recipe for a long time. "I spent a long time formulating my recipe."

"Top secret, huh?" she teased, rocking on the balls of her feet.

"Yes."

She didn't like the way he said the word. It shut her out and made her feel worse than Andretti's sneering comment had yesterday.

Keith continued working on the machines as Teddi grew quiet. She stood there a full minute, chewing on her lip, telling herself she was an idiot. Finally she walked from the room.

"Where're you going?" he called, looking up.

"Since you want to play James Bond with your chocolate, I have a wall to see to." With that, she began painting the last wall in the front room.

She splashed a rollerful of paint on the wall. So he had his chocolate and she had her dancing. She beat down the bubble of beige she had splattered on the wall. They knew just where they stood with each other. Her strokes became less fierce. Or did they?

"Missouri?"

"Yes?" she answered after a beat.

"Why are you beating the wall with the roller?"

"It's called therapy."

"It's called making dents in the wall." He wiped the grease from his fingers. He stood in the doorway for a moment, watching her. Her chin was jutting out again. "I didn't mean to hurt your feelings," he said quietly.

So he wasn't as insensitive as she thought. She moved her shoulders, feigning indifference. She didn't turn around. "You've got your chocolate and I've got my dancing. Everybody's entitled to an obsession."

How about two? he wondered, watching the way her body moved as the roller glided along the wall.

What was he going to do about the way he felt about her? he wondered, totally confounded. A whining sound from the other room broke the uncomfortable silence.

"I think one of your machines is calling you."

Keith walked back into the kitchen, leaving Teddi frowning to herself.

For the next few days, Teddi found herself avoiding Keith, afraid of triggering something off within herself. She had successfully shut away her feelings. She concentrated on the front room and on her dance routines. The following week she was at the newsstand, eagerly asking for the new copy of *Variety*. The man recognized her and clucked as he took her money.

"Still knocking your head against a wall, eh?"

"I'm a slow learner." She grinned at the old man behind the magazines as she took the paper. But her grin slipped away as she thumbed through the pages. This week there was nothing.

"Any luck?" Keith asked her when he walked into the store that afternoon. She was perched on a ladder, busily stenciling.

She didn't look down. "Nobody's auditioning dancers this week."

He walked up to the ladder. Her toes were curled around the step she was on. He felt an urge to kiss each one. The war that had raged within him for an entire week was finally wearing down his barriers. She haunted him even when he wasn't with her. And when she was, he wanted her more each time he saw her. "What are you doing?"

"Giving you a trademark," she answered pertly. "How do you like it?" A delicate line of chocolate angels encircled one wall.

He couldn't keep from touching her. He ran his hand along her long, slender leg. Hunger flamed in him. "I don't remember discussing this."

"That's because you didn't." He had kept his distance for the past few days, and she had thought that perhaps Friday night had been some sort of an aberration. His slightest touch told her it wasn't. She could *feel* his desire. "I can't paint when you do that."

"Good," he said. "Don't paint."

She looked down at him. Something leaped within her chest, but she forced it away. Only fools made the same mistake twice. "Don't you like my angels?"

"I like the angel on my ladder much better." He stepped back. "Come down, Missouri." His voice was low.

She put the stencil down on top of the ladder. Holding on to both sides to steady herself, she descended slowly. He was so handsome it hurt. Her voice quavered as she looked up into his face. "Yes?"

He was about to tell her he loved her. Something had caught at his throat when he had seen her up there, straining to get the last angel just right. But at the last minute, fear erased the words. Instead he just took her into his arms and kissed her.

Fire flared between them. Teddi had no idea who was the cause. It was just there, as it had been last week. Her head began to swim.

The knocking became insistent.

"Is that my heart or yours?" Keith asked, reluctantly raising his lips from hers. She was more potent than the strongest liquor.

"It's the door." As reason returned, she greeted it reluctantly. Insanity, when brought on by Keith, had so much more going for it.

"I'm not having anything else delivered," he said. He lowered his mouth to hers.

The knock came again.

With a strong sigh, he took her hand and went to the door.

In the doorway stood a proper-looking man in a white shirt and bow tie. There wasn't a bead of perspiration on him, Teddi noticed.

"Yes?" Keith asked impatiently.

There was a single-word reply. "Peabody."

"Yes?" Keith repeated himself.

"Board of Health." It looked as if it agonized Peabody to explain anything.

"Board of—oh." Had he forgotten this, too? No, he specifically recalled that the Board of Health inspector was due Friday. "Mr. Peabody, you're not supposed to come until the end of the week."

Peabody didn't move. Though slight, he looked formidable. "My office specifically set up an appointment for—" he haughtily took out his appointment book from his shirt pocket "your establishment on Tuesday, July..." His voice trailed off. The frown on his lips made him look like a discontented troll. "You're not Miles Tavern."

Keith released a sigh of relief. "No, we're not."

Peabody turned on his heel. "Friday at ten," he shot over his shoulder.

Oscar Peabody didn't like making mistakes. It showed in his attitude when he returned on Friday. Rather than blame himself, he was wont to blame anyone handy—in this case, Keith and his kitchen.

Keith got the uneasy feeling that this was not going to be a picnic, even though his kitchen was immaculate. He and Teddi had worked into the wee hours of the morning, making sure that everything was beyond reproach.

They could have eaten off the floors.

Peabody looked disdainfully around the kitchen. "There's nothing I hate more than sloppy food establishments."

"You're absolutely right," Teddi agreed, coming between Keith and Peabody. She was wearing a light pink sundress that flattered her every curve. Her tanned bare legs were shod in flat open-toed sandals. Mr. Peabody, she had noted, was short. He also appeared to be rather humorless. She didn't trust people who couldn't laugh, or at least smile. She had already decided that Keith was going to need help.

Peabody gave her a look that would wither lesser people. All Teddi did was smile innocently. He went around the kitchen slowly, his clipboard in one hand as he ran his other hand along everything. A smudge of dirt was evident in the corner. He scribbled something down on his clipboard. "The law allows for a certain percentage of hairs and rodent wastes to be mixed in with food.'' It was plain by his expression that the law might allow for it, but he didn't.

"That's disgusting," Teddi chimed in, taking Peabody's arm solicitously. "They really shouldn't."

A lone brow rose painfully high on the wide forehead. "Nice to see someone agrees with my standards."

"Mr. Calloway sets nothing but the highest standards," Teddi told him solemnly.

She's not a dancer, Keith thought, watching her performance with a mixture of amusement and bewilderment. She's an actress.

"What's that?"

Her heart skipped a beat as she saw Peabody's eyes narrow. Her breath returned when she saw the object of his question. Teddi crossed over to the chair. "Oh, those." She scooped the shoes up. "These are my tap shoes." How *could* she have forgotten to pick those up? she berated herself.

"Dancer?" he asked, his tour momentarily forgotten.

How the hell could they have overlooked her shoes? Keith thought irritably. He remembered she had had them in her hand when she had come down to help. "Mr. Peabody, if you'll notice that there is no—" Keith began in an attempt to show him just how immaculate his kitchen was.

Peabody waved a thin, temperamental hand at Keith without bothering to look in his direction. "Later, Calloway. You were saying?" he asked Teddi.

"Yes, I'm a dancer. But there aren't that many musicals to audition for."

The frown deepened to one of disgust. Teddi wondered if she had made a blunder. "They don't make musicals like they used to," Peabody grumbled. "Why, I can remember taking my late wife to a production of *Kismet* with Alfred Drake. Those were songs in those days. They had words, melodies."

A true believer, Teddi thought, overjoyed. She smiled. He was hers.

Keith stared as the tight-lipped little man became animated right before his eyes. Before long, he and Teddi were discussing movies that had been produced in the fifties and exchanging trivia information. During the discussion, Teddi asked Keith to bring down some of his chocolate for Peabody to sample. As he went, Keith wondered vaguely when they had changed places.

The clock over the grinder ticked the hour away. Keith sat on the butcher-block counter, listening to the two talk. Peabody was actually smiling, he marveled.

Finally, Peabody rose.

"It's a pleasure meeting you, Miss McKay. Don't forget, I want tickets when you land in a show."

"Count on it," Teddi drawled.

Keith raised a brow. Her voice had slipped into a twang that sounded as if it originated south of the Mason-Dixon Line, not Missouri. She was a charmer; there was no doubt about it.

"Mr. Calloway." Peabody regained some of his reserve as he turned to Keith. "You'll be hearing from the board within a few days. Possibly a week." He moved his shoulders. "You know how slowly government wheels turn."

"And what will I be hearing from them?" Keith asked, walking the man to the door.

Peabody rested his hand on top of the clipboard. "That you appear to have one of the cleanest establishments in New York City, barring a little dust here and there that I'm sure will be taken care of by the time you open." He smiled at Teddi, then turned to Keith. "By the way—" he bit off another piece of chocolate, then waved the remainder to make his point "—your chocolate's excellent."

He marched off. Keith didn't even bother to watch him go. Instead he whisked Teddi up into his arms, whirling her around. The man had entered his store smarting from his mistake and looking for any infringement to mark down against Keith. He left smiling and humming a song from *My Fair Lady*. It was all thanks to her. "The State Department could use you," he said with a laugh, nuzzling Teddi's neck.

Just so long as you can, she thought as she wrapped her arms around his neck.

Nine

––––––

He had felt like a fifth wheel. Sitting there and listening to her talk to the health inspector about movies earlier that afternoon, Keith had felt shut out of Teddi's world. Nothing seemed straightforward anymore. He began to pour his first batch of chocolate into the tiny molds, his mind on Teddi. His simple desire to help her wasn't simple at all; helping her would probably mean losing her.

He finished pouring and set the bowl down.

Didn't loving someone mean you wanted to see her happy at all costs? He wondered if he was truly that unselfish. He wrestled with his thoughts as he set a tray of angels aside. What he no longer wrestled with was the idea of loving her. He had come to terms with that rather easily once he had let himself accept the fact. It was the rest of it that was hard to accept. Loving someone meant opening up your heart to risks, risks he had never taken before.

As they worked now, Teddi plied him with questions about his avocation. He wasn't altogether sure what motivated her, or how to react to it. He had never met anyone so curious about his dream before. Still hesitant about parting with his formula, he spoke in vague terms, telling her that the secret in making excellent chocolate lay in working with small batches, which were lovingly attended to and made without any preservatives.

He noticed that her spirits flagged as the day wore on. He was sure it was because she still hadn't found any work. He promised himself to do what he could.

Even though he dreaded it, he called Emily later that evening.

He dialed, and after three rings, a very cold, metallic voice answered. "Hello?"

He could visualize her. Dark hair pulled back in a tight knot at the base of her neck. A few stubborn unruly strands making her seem just a tad disorganized. Sensible glasses. "Hi, Emily, it's me." When there was a pause with no recognition on her end, he said, "Keith."

"How are you?" The tone was formal. Ever since her husband had left her, Emily had sounded like their father: distant, removed. Cold. He was tempted to hang up. He thought of Teddi and pressed on.

"I'm fine, Em."

He could almost hear her stiffen. "Please don't call me that." Jim had always referred to her that way.

"I did when we were children."

"We're not children any longer."

"No—" he shifted uncomfortably in his chair "—we're not. Listen, Em—ily," he added, though it was an effort, "I'll keep this short."

"Fine."

He wondered if only children knew how fortunate they were. "Do you still keep in touch with any of the old crowd?"

"What do you mean by 'old crowd'?"

She sounded like a stereotypical schoolmarm. He could remember a time when she had been a lot warmer, a lot more human. "The people Jim used to hang out with."

"No," she said sharply. "My work takes up all my time."

He tried again. "Look, Emily, the truth is that I'm trying to do a favor for a friend. She's a dancer and she needs a break."

"And you want to know who she should sleep with to get a part."

He sat up, ramrod-straight. He had had enough. "No, damn it! Em—"

"Emily!"

"Em!" he repeated with feeling. "Get off your damn high horse. You're not the only woman who's been burned. Don't compound your mistake by turning into a cold-blooded creature like Father."

"How nice of you to call and show concern." The words were etched in ice.

He was ready to slam down the phone. That wouldn't help Missouri, he told himself. His grip on the receiver tightened. "*Do* you know anyone who could help her? I need a name, an introduction. Something."

There was a long pause. "You, too, Keith?"

The tone sounded a little like the old Emily, the one who had always haplessly garnered their parents' displeasure. The social ugly duckling their paternal grandmother turned her nose up at.

He ran his hand through his hair, sinking back. "Yeah, me, too."

"Watch your money."

"I don't have to." She'd take that as a direct insult on her own choice, he realized, and added quickly, "It's all tied up in chocolate."

"That's right. Kent told me what you were up to."

He hadn't seen his eldest brother since last Christmas. "Have you seen much of him lately?"

"Now and again." She sighed. "Listen, Keith, I'll see what I can do. But I doubt it'll be anything."

"Thanks." A dial tone met his ear. Keith replaced the phone in its cradle. That had been the most civil conversation he and Emily had had in five years. He felt sorry for her. He had always felt sorry for her. After her breakup he had tried to come to her aid, but she was too bitter, too unapproachable, to let him in. And so he had retreated from her, as he had from all his family. Poor old Em, always looking for love.

Now, he mused, Emily had an important position as a chemist and Kent and Edward were stockbrokers. And their father was satisfied with three-fourths of his family.

Keith sat looking at the phone. He hoped Emily would come through.

"It's not ready yet?" Teddi asked, watching the giant blade slowly turn within the metal pot, mixing the ingredients that Keith had spent the better part of yesterday fussing over. "How long does it take?" She tapped the side of the vibrating machine.

"Three days."

She followed him as he gathered up his expense sheets. The numbers, he thought, were overwhelming.

"Three days?" she echoed. "Just for chocolate?"

"For *my* chocolate."

She caught just the barest hint of arrogance in his voice. Professional pride, she thought, allowing for it. She had it, too. "Can't you speed it up?"

He looked up, a smile playing on his lips. "What's the matter, sweet tooth bothering you?"

She leaned over the table on her elbows and cupped her face in her hands. "No, but I thought if you could have a big batch ready, you could take it to the show."

"Missouri—" he put down his pencil "—what are you talking about?"

She sat down on the edge of the table. "The show at Madison Square Garden. I read about it in the newspaper this morning after you left for work.

They're having a chocolate lovers' convention start-
ing tomorrow, and I thought that maybe—''

He held up his hand. "I know about the show, but
it's just impossible for me to have a booth. Some
things can't be rushed. They need time."

She smiled to herself. She certainly hadn't. She
thought she would, but it had happened just the
same—like lightning. Aloud she asked, "So, can't you
whip up a batch to put on display?"

He reached for her hand. "Tell me," he said, pulling her onto his lap. "What makes you such an ex-
pert in marketing?" He curled a strand of her hair
around his finger.

His other hand rested lightly on her thigh. Teddi felt
the warmth spreading inside her. "I had an uncle who
was a salesman. He taught me that nothing's ever
gained if you just lean back and let things slide."

Keith cupped the back of her head. "Might be
something to that." He turned her face toward him
and kissed her.

Teddi's lips parted, inviting the delicious taste that
only he could offer her. As his kiss deepened, her arms
went around his neck, her body straining for more.

He was never going to have enough of her, no matter what he told himself. When she was around, he
couldn't think clearly, couldn't function right. He
would be his old self for several moments, and then
he'd think of her mouth, or the way her body had felt
against his, and he'd be lost again.

He put his hands beneath her blouse, lightly graz-
ing her warm, supple skin. How he wanted her. Every

fiber in his body cried out for him to take her, right here, right now. She pulled out of him feelings, emotions, sensations, that he never dreamed existed.

Teddi could feel her desire building, could feel her need for him reaching out. She always needed more, and she never had enough. Behind her, the rumbling hum of the mixing machine vaguely penetrated her consciousness as her mind focused on his lips and how they reduced every part of her to liquid fire.

When she left, there was going to be an unbearable gap in his life. He had to divorce himself from wanting her, from aching this way, whenever his thoughts turned to her. His hand dropped, and his head moved back.

Her lips felt softly blurred, the impression of his lips still on them. She struggled to get her mind into order. "So, are you going to the convention?"

He couldn't help holding on to her waist. How could a creature so light, so delicate, do this to him? Imprison him this way? "Wouldn't miss it for the world. Want to come?"

She rested her forehead against his. "Do they give out free samples?"

"It would be inhuman not to," he said, chuckling.

"Then I'll come."

He let his finger glide slowly down her arm. Teddi stifled a shiver that waltzed through her. "They don't know what they're in for. Now it you'll get your lovely weight off me, I have some work to do."

Teddi obliged, feeling put out as she did so. He was acting like a cordial friend. When he kissed her, she had thought that she felt a need there akin to her own. Yet he had pulled back, cutting the kiss short and ending it in levity. Was he trying to subtly tell her that although what they had had was pleasant, there was no room for her in his life?

She went out into the front room and back to her stencils. Climbing the ladder, she berated herself for being such a romantic. Second place to chocolate, that was the position she had taken—if even that. No promises had passed between them. He had been planning to attend the convention, yet he hadn't mentioned it to her. If she hadn't brought it up, would he have gone alone? Without her? He was shutting her out again.

She picked up the thin paintbrush and then outlined another chocolate cherub. Three weeks ago she hadn't known this man existed, and both her mind and her virginity had been intact. Now she had given him the most precious thing she could—herself—and had given up her peace of mind, as well.

Muttering to herself as her stroke smeared over the outline, she pulled out the rag that she had tucked into her waistband and quickly erased the telltale smudge before it dried. Be a big girl, Teddi. These things happen. People meet, they become attracted to each other, they make love and they go on with their lives.

People might, but she didn't. No, by God, she didn't. She set a high price tag on what had passed between them.

The angel turned out slightly crooked.

* * *

The smell of chocolate was everywhere. Teddi, dressed in a form-fitting navy sheath, held on to Keith's arm lightly as they walked around the huge hall. She had never seen so much chocolate in her life. And there were groups of people lining up everywhere to sample all they could. Every big name was represented, as well as countless smaller, independent entrepreneurs. Looking the place over, Teddi got the same feeling she had when she had seen the long line of dancers at the Grayson Theater.

"God, just look at them all." She looked at Keith. "Doesn't it intimidate you just a little?"

"No," he said cheerfully, snaring a piece of chocolate for her as they walked.

She accepted it with a smile. He sounded just like her. They had this much in common, she thought. Faith in themselves. Maybe the rest would work itself out. "You know, *you* should be here."

"I am."

"You know what I mean," she said impatiently. "You should have a table here." She paused to dip a strawberry into a pool of chocolate that sprang from a chocolate fountain in the shape of Bacchus, the god of wine. She was so impressed with the structure that for a moment she lost her train of thought. She stood back, staring at the dark statue. "I guess they don't have a god of chocolate," she quipped.

"Maybe you could come up with one in your spare time. Another trademark." Keith grinned at her, steadying her hand as she offered him the remainder of the chocolate-covered strawberry.

His lips brushed her fingertips. When would they make love again? she wondered, feeling the need rise within her. "This chocolate doesn't hold a candle to yours," she said as they moved on.

"That's what I like, unbiased loyalty."

"Well, it's true. You know, if you had worked quicker, you could have had your chocolate ready for this show."

He stepped back to let two women pass between them. "I couldn't get the equipment on time."

She wouldn't let the subject drop. "What about the batch you have in your apartment?"

A woman in a white rabbit costume walked by with a tray covered with white chocolate rabbits. Keith took two and handed one to Teddi. "I hardly think that fifty pieces would have made a dent in this crowd."

"That's all you have left?" she asked, surprised.

"That's all."

She stopped moving through the throng. Something wasn't making sense. "Where did you make them?"

"Same place I perfected my formula. At Venus Chocolates. I worked there summers while I was at school. The supervisor there let me fool around with the equipment during off hours."

She cocked her head. "Was that legal?"

He gave her a beguiling, boyish grin. "Arnold and I didn't discuss legalities. I reminded him of the son he had lost."

The chocolate rabbit disappeared between her lips. "When did you stop working there?"

He marveled how she could eat and still talk clearly. "Three years ago."

It still wasn't making sense to her. "The angels I had didn't taste three years old."

He took her elbow, guiding her to a particular table. "That was done at great expense. I rented the facilities this time, just to see if the formula held up the way I thought it did."

"And it did." It wasn't a question.

"It did, but I couldn't go on using the facilities. As it was, Arnold had to pull strings and call in favors just to arrange for me to make the batch I have at home."

His explanation seemed to satisfy her. She eyed the table he had led her to. An inviting pyramid of dark chocolate met the eye, while rows of chocolate drops outlined the table. Behind them, just to the left, there was a cooking demonstration going on. Lots and lots of chocolate, she thought.

"What's the purpose of all this?" Teddi asked, gesturing around. "Besides having the local population break out and gain weight, I mean."

He wasn't listening to her. Keith was sampling the tiny morsel of chocolate he had picked up at a nearby table. He rolled it around in his mouth. It was unbelievably delectable and tasted, he realized, a lot like his own. But not quite, he decided, his smile restored. "What?"

"Is this convention just for its own sake, for the manufacturers to meet one another and shoot the breeze?"

She reduced everything to simple terms, he thought. "No, it's for the competition to feel one another out. And it's for new enterprises like mine to display their wares and perhaps, if they're lucky, gain some financial backers. There's a lot of money to be made in chocolate." He pointed out a rather heavyset man sampling a piece of a chocolate gingerbread house in the far corner. "Take him, for instance. That's Andrew DuBois. He writes for *The Chocolate Fancier* magazine. A good word from him and a new chocolate empire is launched."

"A good word from him, huh?" She studied the bearded man in the white suit. She watched him move slowly from table to table, stopping to exchange a few words and take a sample with him.

Keith turned his attention to the display in the center of the room. It was a replica of the Statue of Liberty, done entirely in milk chocolate. "You know, I've never seen Miss Liberty look quite this delicious before. Hope the air conditioning holds out. If it starts melting, you might be called on to do a mercy eating." He turned to look at Teddi. She was no longer next to him. "Missouri?" What table had captured her? he wondered, looking around the crowded hall. Why did he have this uneasy feeling when he lost sight of her? It wasn't as if she couldn't take care of herself. She wasn't a child.

He forced himself to concentrate on the reason he was there: to see how good the competition was and to get ready for the next convention, which would be in Dallas in two months.

It wasn't until he was in front of his fifth display that he caught sight of Teddi again. She wasn't alone. He stopped in his tracks... forgetting the sample he held in his hand.

"It'll melt if you hold on to it too long," the man behind the table told him. He motioned with his hands, and Keith placed the chocolate in his mouth.

What was she up to now? Weaving in and out of lines in order to reach her, he quickly crossed the room.

"Oh, here he is now," she said as if he were appearing on cue. She extended her hand to Keith. "Keith, this is Mr. DuBois of *The Chocolate Fancier*."

"I know," Keith said between clenched teeth.

"Miss McKay—" the portly man began.

"Teddi," she corrected him, smiling broadly.

The little eyes nearly disappeared as the beard spread out in a warm smile. "Teddi has been telling me a lot about your chocolate. I must say, what I sampled is heavenly."

"You *sampled* some of my chocolate?" Keith asked incredulously. "How—?" His eyes narrowed as he looked at Teddi.

The smile she gave him had all the guile of a newborn babe.

"I realize, of course, that you're not properly set up yet, but I thought that perhaps I could give your establishment a visit, say, at the end of next week. Teddi tells me that you'll be in business then."

"I'm afraid—" Keith began.

"That that might be too far in the future," Teddi cut in. "We'll be ready for you by next Wednesday. Here's the address." She pressed a piece of paper into his palm. She had written out the address on several pieces of paper before she had left the shop.

DuBois tucked the note into his pocket, his eyes never leaving Teddi. "Next Wednesday, then. Shall we say around one?"

"Perfect," Teddi agreed.

"Now if you'll excuse me," DuBois began, "duty calls." He lumbered off to another booth.

Keith took hold of her arm—rather tightly, she thought. "Whose business is this, Missouri?" he whispered against her ear.

"Yours," she said innocently.

"Then why aren't you letting me run it? And how did he get a sample of my chocolate?"

"From me."

He closed his eyes, searching for strength. "I realize that, but how—"

"I brought some." She patted the drawstring purse in her hand. "I took a few angels out of the cupboard while you were getting ready in the other room. Keith, you're not going to get anywhere dragging your feet."

"I'm not dragging my feet, Missouri. But I'm not exactly ready to free-fall, either. Suppose the batch I'm working on doesn't turn out?"

There was no supposing that. "It will," she assured him, patting his cheek.

He found her simple faith confounding.

"You shouldn't have cornered him without saying something to me," he said to her as they walked back into the shop. They had been arguing about her burst of enthusiasm ever since they had left the convention.

She turned, her hand on the doorknob. "Would you have let me talk to him if you'd known what I was up to?"

"No."

"I rest my case." She took a piece of chocolate out of her bag and began to eat it.

"Missouri, you don't have a case."

She turned, her eyes searching his. She dropped her purse, crammed full of chocolates, onto the floor. "Maybe not. Not when you're so pigheaded."

"What are you talking about?"

"Never mind." She marched off into the kitchen. "Let's check on your mixer." Why was he being so stubborn? She was only trying to help. What was wrong with him?

The mixer was still rumbling, just as it had been for the past two days. "Are you sure it isn't ready yet?" She touched the chocolate splattered on the inside of the rim.

Keith grabbed her hand and pulled it back. "Be careful. You could get your finger cut off."

"Don't worry. It won't spoil the taste," she said angrily.

"I was thinking of you."

"That's a novelty."

He still held her hand raised in the air. "Look, maybe I've been a little testy today—"

"*Maybe?* Compared to you, Attila the Hun is even tempered."

"Sorry."

"I'll think about accepting your apology."

"You're dripping," he observed. Before she could respond, he brought her hand to his lips and slowly licked the chocolate away.

She wanted to stay angry; anger helped her maintain her defenses against him. But it was hard to stay angry when she felt everything inside her disintegrating. What was with him? He ran cold one minute, hot the next. It was becoming unbearably hot as his teeth nipped at her knuckles.

All hell broke loose within her.

Ten

It was as if she had been waiting for nothing else these past few days. Her entire being had been on hold, waiting for his touch. Just like Snow White, asleep in her crystal casket, waiting for her prince, she thought. She was being romantic again, but she didn't care. She loved the sentiment, the feeling, him. Nothing else mattered.

There was a burning need inside her. As a torrent of passion surfaced, she permitted herself to be swept away with it, luxuriating in the taste, the feel, the scent of him.

She made him feel vulnerable, defenseless. There was none of the detached, safe feelings he normally experienced in a relationship. His senses might have been aroused when he had been with other women, but not his emotions, not his mind. No one had ever claimed those before. He had never been so involved, so totally absorbed. She had managed to fill every bit of him, leaving room for nothing else.

The realization scared the hell out of him even as ecstasy took hold.

Perhaps it had been the near argument. Or perhaps it was the intense passion he felt in her kiss. Whatever had prompted it, this time he couldn't hold on to any semblance of control, couldn't wait until he had carried her upstairs to his bed. As their lips met again and again and their bodies pressed together, hard, heated, wanting, he pulled her down to the floor.

"I want you now, Missouri. Now."

She opened her eyes. The irises were clouded with desire. Her breathing was heavy as a smile curved her lips. "Good. This would be an awful time," she murmured, her fingers pulling his shirt up over his shoulders, "to tell me that you've decided to work on your chocolate." The shirt came off. Her hands spread, spanning the hard muscles along his back. Her heart hammered in her ears.

He laughed as he kissed her cheek. With his tongue, he lightly traced the curve down to her mouth. The kiss deepened, as did his sense of urgency.

He didn't want to take her roughly, but it was all he could do to keep from tearing her dress from her body. He needed to touch her, to make her his.

His teeth, tongue and lips created havoc at the hollow of her neck; his hands burrowed behind her, searching for her zipper. "You're overdressed."

"For the occasion, yes." She felt his lips form a smile against her skin. She tottered on the brink of mindless passion, wanting desperately to memorize everything before her mind slipped away. She arched her hips as he slipped her dress down, exposing her breasts. She sucked in her breath as he possessed the supple fullness with his hand, his thumb teasing her nipple until it was taut, aching. Her head began to whirl. She dug her fingers into his bare shoulders.

He was losing himself in her. He had no identity, no sense of where he ended and she began; he was part of a circle. She made him feel complete. He couldn't—wouldn't—let her go out of his life. He heard her moan, which increased his own desire, his own needs. She wanted him as much as he wanted her.

His hands were everywhere at once, touching, caressing, inflaming. She glided into each touch, wanting, needing more. The feel of his tongue as it caressed her breasts sent her on her journey toward the summit again. She could feel herself lifting, floating, half languid, half frenzied. An unbelievable combination, yet it was happening to her.

With no barriers left between them, she could feel his body heating, her own responding as first his hand and then his mouth covered the sensitive area where her thigh met the rest of the body. Her eyes flew open as the first strings of ecstasy were strummed.

She moaned his name in a voice he had never heard before. It smoldered, half pleading, half crying. Still he continued, working her into a frenzy, using only his lips, his tongue.

She hadn't known it could be like this, where pleasure was almost pain. Without knowing, she pressed him against her, her fingers winding tightly into his hair. Crest after crest was met, each explosion leading her to a higher plateau. She couldn't stop trembling.

And then he was over her again, his face blotting out the little light in the room, blotting out the world. He *was* her world.

She had no breath left as he took her almost savagely. He couldn't hold back any longer. He needed her, and the need still frightened him. The smell of chocolate mingled with the delectable fragrance of her skin. Keith stopped thinking altogether.

His ragged breathing hissed against her ear. It was the most beautiful sound she had ever heard. He cared. At this moment, he cared. Later she'd deal with tomorrow, with facts, with being second in his life. Today, right now, he was hers, and that was all that mattered.

When he took her, it was like sailing into the curve of a hurricane. She had never felt so exhilarated, so spent. And content. Oh, so content.

I love you, she mouthed against his ear, the words still trapped within her mouth. Even in her dazed state, she knew that saying them aloud would make him withdraw. And she never wanted him to withdraw. She'd move heaven and earth to keep him happy, to keep him hers.

Gradually, although her body was willing to spend the rest of its days beneath him, savoring his weight over her, her mind began to register the fact that the floor was hard.

Just a little longer, her body pleaded.

He moved, balancing his weight on his elbows. Dark blue eyes searched her face. "Did I hurt you, Missouri?" he asked.

His voice was so kind, so tender, she felt an ache well up in her throat. She framed his face in her hands. "You could never hurt me." She raised her head to kiss his lips.

He felt aroused all over again. How could it be possible? What kind of a spell did she cast over him? "Missouri, this'll only start—"

Her grin spread wide, her lips a fraction of an inch away. "What'll it start?"

He couldn't help himself, didn't want to. "This." He took her mouth again, knowing as he did so that a million times from now wouldn't be enough. She had spoiled him for anyone else.

They slept in his bed. Teddi told him that hers was hard and lumpy. She murmured that with her first paycheck, she intended to buy a new bed, one that didn't fold up into a sofa.

He stroked her thigh with slow, deliberate caresses, while his fingers memorized every curve. "I'll raise your rent," Keith told her.

"Why?"

"So you'll have to go on sleeping here."

She curled happily against his side. "Sounds good to me. You plow your money back into chocolate and I plow mine into—" she raised her face to be level with his "—pleasure."

He caught her lips and kissed her with the tender awareness that love brought.

The phone rang, interrupting a deepening kiss before it swept them both away. Teddi fell back against the pillow with a happy sigh as Keith jerked up the receiver. "Yes?" he snapped.

There was no answer for a moment. And then, "Keith?"

"Emily?" He leaned over Teddi and looked at the clock on his nightstand. What was she doing, calling him at eleven o'clock at night? Emily was a firm believer in the early-to-bed-early-to-rise edict.

"You got lucky. I have a name for you."

"A name?" he mumbled dumbly.

Teddi sat up and began nibbling on his shoulder. Keith's mind began clouding again.

"For that friend of yours. The dancer."

Friend. They had gone beyond that stage several weeks ago. Maybe even from the first moment. "Terrific." He opened the drawer, rooting around for a paper and pencil.

"He's a producer—Lawrence Morrison. He just arrived in town, and he's got a show together that looks as if it's going to be bound for Broadway. Jim used to be one of his gofers."

Just how good was the man? He didn't want to raise Missouri's hopes for no reason. He hated the way disappointment reflected in her eyes. "Em, why didn't he ever give Jim a job?" Keith asked.

The words came slowly, as if they were costing her. "He tried, but Jim wasn't any good really. He just made wonderful conversation. Jim could hold an audience in the palm of his hand as long as they were sipping from martini glasses." She paused. "Have your 'friend' tell Morrison Emily Healy sent her. Morrison has a good memory for names. It might do some good. By the way, you've something in common. The man's a chocoholic."

"Em, you're a doll," Keith cried. "What's his number?"

Emily told him that Morrison was staying at the Plaza Hotel and gave him a room number. "Good luck, Keith. I hope it works out for you."

"Thanks, Em. I know this wasn't easy for you."

"No," his sister agreed, "it wasn't." The line went dead.

"What was all that about?" Teddi asked.

"That was my sister."

"I gathered that. I thought you two didn't speak."

"We don't, normally."

Teddi drew back, studying him. She pulled the sheet up, covering herself. She felt a wedge being formed between them again. "You're not going to tell me, are you?"

He took her shoulders and slid her back down onto the bed. "Nope."

Before she had a chance to protest, he covered her mouth with his. And just before her mind slipped into a flaming haze, she thought that she still hadn't penetrated his inner core. He still had secrets from her.

It hurt.

It was incredibly simple, Keith thought the next day. All he had done was call the hotel and ask for Morrison's room. He had gotten the man himself. Within five minutes, he had an appointment. Of course, somehow or other, he had allowed the man to believe that he was interested in investing in his show. That was how the meeting was arranged. Keith showed up at the Plaza an hour after he pulled his cab into the dispatch office. He had stopped home long enough to change and leave a confused Teddi staring after his departing figure. He had told her that he had a meeting with a possible investor. That explained the three-piece pearl-gray suit and Wedgwood-blue shirt. She had offered to change and go with him—almost insisted on it—but he had convinced her to stay and watch the chocolate. The machine had to be turned off at a precise time. With his chocolate, timing, as well as temperature and selection, was everything.

Grumbling, Teddi complied. He kissed her pouting lips and left.

Now he was standing in the hotel suite, waiting for Lawrence Morrison to get off the phone. As a pièce de résistance, Keith had brought along a few of his chocolates, neatly arranged in a blue box. Leave no stone unturned, he told himself.

He watched the short, balding man in the four-hundred-dollar suit grow dramatic as he rose on his toes. He gestured with his cigar, the gestures becoming more and more exaggerated. Obviously, Keith thought, pretending not to notice, the conversation wasn't going well. The observation was reinforced when Morrison slammed the receiver down.

As he approached Keith, the deep frown on Morrison's face turned into an instant smile. If sharks could smile, they'd look like that, Keith thought. He probably thinks he's going to talk me out of a lot of money.

"That was unavoidable." Morrison nodded toward the phone as he took Keith's hand into both of his. An enormous ruby on his pinky gleamed, catching the afternoon light. His hand went back to free his mouth of the long cigar. "So, what can I get you, Mr. Calloway? Room service is pretty damn good here."

"Nothing, thanks." Quickly Keith searched for the best way to approach the man. His mind was shamefully devoid of any concrete plan.

"What's that?" Bushy brows rose as Morrison looked at the small blue box under Keith's arm.

"Chocolate." Keith presented it to him. "My sister says you've a sweet tooth for chocolate."

"Your sister?" For a moment, he reached into his mind to try to remember the details of his early-morning conversation. "Oh, yes, Emily. Bless her heart, she remembered." He sat down on a chair, his stomach spreading out like hasty pudding. He smiled down at the chocolate. "Angels, eh? Very appropriate, seeing as how theater investors are called angels."

He opened his mouth wide and managed to consume an entire angel in one bite. His expression changed from genial to intrigued. "Say, this is really good. And I ought to know." He patted his immense stomach. "Pack away a lot of chocolate, I do." He picked up another angel and turned it around. "Who'd you say this was by?"

"I didn't. They're mine." Keith leaned forward. "Now, Mr. Morrison, I think I'd better explain—" He was going to have to clear the air. Morrison, he surmised, was a man who appreciated honesty. He was looking less like a shark by the minute.

"Yours?" Morrison looked down at the angel in his hand. This time he bit the wing contemplatively. The result was even better than before. He leaned forward, bringing the back legs of the chair slightly off the carpet. "Let me get this straight. You *make* these?"

At any other time, Keith would have been delighted to talk about his chocolate. But right now he wanted to get on about Missouri. "Yes, I do."

Crafty brows knitted together. "Have you got a backer, boy?" He saw dollar signs.

"No, I don't," Keith said slowly. "I'm just getting started. As a matter of fact, I'm opening my shop in about a week. But back to the reason for my being here—"

Morrison shook his head. "Boy, I don't want your money. You're going to need it to finance these angels. As a matter of fact—" he cocked his head, the thick neck overflowing his preposterously stiff collar "—I just might be convinced to do a little investing in your business myself." He touched his bulbous nose, which appeared to have connected with at least one fist during its lifetime. "I've got a nose for success, boy. I can smell it about you."

Keith sat back, stunned. "You—you want to invest in my business?"

Morrison planted his palms on his pant legs with a swat. "That's what I said. Show business isn't the only thing I'm into. Tell you what. You give me the address of your place and I'll have my accountant out there the first of the week to check everything. If he likes your operation, you've got yourself a backer." He grinned broadly, digging into the blue box. "I want a batch of these at my hotel room next week. Fair enough?" Another angel disappeared forever.

"Fair?" Keith repeated. Morrison's offer was coming at a time when Keith's cash reserves were seriously dwindling. The cost of refurbishing had been more than he had anticipated, even with his doing most of the work himself. And the price of importing his special cocoa beans had jumped. He felt gratified and overwhelmed at this stroke of luck.

But, he reminded himself, he was here for Missouri, not for himself. "Mr. Morrison, I have to be honest with you."

"Honesty's the best policy, boy," Morrison muttered, dabbing his finger along the edges of the box to pick up any chocolate crumbs he might have missed. His mind wasn't on Keith at the moment.

"I came because I have this friend." Lover? Neither title covered her, he realized, not completely. She was so much more to him now. "And she needs a break."

Morrison looked up, saying nothing.

"She's a dancer, and this new show of yours—"

"Is a musical comedy." Morrison nodded thoughtfully.

Was he going to send him out? Keith wondered. Had he blown a good thing?

"Is she any good?"

"Terrific," Keith lied. He'd never even seen her dance, he realized. But now was no time to admit that.

The burly man smacked his lips together. "Anyone who makes chocolate like that—" he tapped the empty box on the coffee table in front of him "—knows talent. We've got one spot in the chorus left. I tell you what. You get me those angels and I'll get her an audition before the others are scheduled." He stuck out his hand. "Deal?"

"Deal." Keith grasped his hand firmly. "I'll not only get you those angels; I'll bring you my favorite chocolate dessert."

"What's that?"

Keith grinned broadly, feeling very content with himself. "Crème de menthe chocolate mousse cake you could die from."

The mountain rose. "I'm looking forward to the funeral, boy."

* * *

"What audition?" Teddi cried, confused. "There isn't anything in the paper about an audition tomorrow." He wasn't making any sense. He had rushed into the store and started talking in mid-sentence. Something, she thought, only she was wont to do.

Keith whirled her around the store. "This is a special one, just for you."

She looked at him suspiciously. "Why?"

"Because Lawrence Morrison is arranging it. He's the producer behind *The Rumpus Room*. And he's also going to invest in my chocolate angels."

"Chocolate Dreams," she corrected, then shook her head. "Run all this by me again."

"Never mind the details. Just go upstairs and practice." He pushed her away from the large vat that was cooking his chocolate mixture. Behind him another batch of chocolate beans had entered the mixer. As the beans tumbled over one another, they created a constant hum.

Teddi's joy was boundless as she ran off to do as he said.

He watched her start to leave. But underneath all this was a nagging feeling he couldn't shake. "Missouri?" he called after her.

One hand braced on the doorknob, she swung around. "Yes?"

"If you get the part, will you be moving out?"

So that was it. Her spirits plummeted. He was doing this so that she'd go. But after what had happened last night? Was he that afraid of commitment, or had she misread all the signs? Tears threatened to spill out.

"Maybe," she tossed over her shoulder, then hurried out. Maybe he needed more money from the apartment, money to put into his business. But if that was the case, why hadn't he just said so?

She stopped, her hand on the banister. The shadows on the wall seemed to echo her uncertainty. No, it was more than that. He wanted her gone, out of his life. There could be no other explanation for why he had gone out of his way like that and talked to this producer. She knew how he felt about the theater. He had made it perfectly clear that first night.

She ran up the stairs two at a time, fighting tears.

Keith looked back at the vat. He'd been right. He had no claim to her, no matter what had happened between them these past few weeks. Once she got what she really wanted, she'd be gone, leaving his life empty. His initial impression about show people returned.

The buzzer went off, reminding him that it was time for the next step. He did it mechanically, his thoughts elsewhere, something he had never done before.

Eleven

The Rusk Theater was within walking distance, if one wanted a long walk. Keith got Nathan to cover for him and took the day off.

As they walked down the street, mingling with the morning throng, Keith kept his fingers laced through Teddi's. It seemed so right, he thought, just walking, holding her hand. As if he had been doing it forever. He knew that fifty years from now he'd want this comfort, this passion coated in contentment.

He was no longer frightened of his need. He had accepted it the way a man might the color of his eyes or the texture of his hair.

What continued to haunt him was the thought of losing her. She had responded to his question of her moving so casually that when it had happened, for a moment he had thought he had misunderstood everything, misjudged, miscalculated on all levels. But when sanity had returned, he knew that he couldn't have been that wrong about what was going on between them.

Yet a basic uncertainty continued to nag at him. He'd never know just what he meant to her until the hurdle was over, until she was in her element and began her career. And here he was, arranging something that might very well be the beginning of the end.

Because he loved her.

"We who are about to die salute you," he thought. A very appropriate sentiment. They continued walking to the theater.

Her shoulder brushed against his arm and he looked at her. Her chin was raised. She looked determined. "Still not nervous?"

She had been too busy wondering whether he had found her a show so that he could get rid of her to be nervous about the audition. She was in top condition, having prepared religiously for the audition, going through her routine until her muscles knew every movement without her conscious direction.

Just as he had become second nature to her, like breathing, she thought with a rueful smile.

"Nope. I either get it, in which case everything's fine, or I don't, in which case I throw myself into your vat of chocolate and die with a smile on my face, mixed in with your secret ingredients."

He picked up on that. "It really bothers you that I won't tell you what I use, doesn't it?"

She lifted her shoulders slightly as they hurried across an avenue. "A little."

He squeezed her hand. "Someday, when the time is right, I'll let you know."

"I'll hold you to that," she promised with a smile, knowing that his revelation would mean that he trusted her completely. There would be no barriers between them then. She wondered if the day would actually come.

They stopped in front of an impressive building, its marquee proclaiming the last few weeks of a smash hit before it went on the road. "Well, this is it." She took three deep, cleansing breaths—not an easy feat, she thought, in New York.

"What's the matter?" Keith asked.

"I'm getting ready."

"Oh, I thought you were hyperventilating."

"That's after, if I get the part."

He nodded and opened the door for her. "I'll keep some champagne and a paper bag waiting." He was reluctant to let her go, and yet he knew he had to. If you love something, set it free. "Break a leg," he called out after her.

He let the door close. Then he stood there, his hand resting against the ornate brass. He'd never even seen her dance. Maybe she wasn't any good. Maybe he was worrying for no reason. Who'd notice him if he sat in the last row and watched?

The man behind the barred ticket cage eyed him suspiciously. "I'm with her," Keith told him, nodding toward the door. "She has an audition." With that, he slipped inside.

Teddi walked down the aisle slowly, the sound of her heels muffled in the deep crimson carpet. Her heart, she realized abruptly, was thumping against her chest. Maybe she *was* nervous. Just a tad.

This is real life, Teddi, she acknowledged. There's a lot to be nervous about.

The man on the stage in the creaseless gray trousers and cream designer pullover did not appear to be in the best of humor.

What is it about these choreographers? she wondered. Were they all monsters? Her knees felt a little weak.

"It's my day off," he said when he saw her. "Make me feel that I gave it up for a good cause."

And hello to you, too, she thought. She took the steps at the side of the stage. "I'm Teddi McKay."

"I *know* who you are, McKay. I wasn't just sitting here hoping some urchin would wander in off the street and treat me to a number out of *Brigadoon.*"

She hesitated, her tap shoes half out of her purse. "I could come back when you're feeling more human."

"Spunk." He nodded, walking around her. He leaned over her. "I detest spunk."

Batting zero, she thought, not blinking as he circled her. She sat down on the lone chair and began putting on her shoes.

"Especially when I'm hungover." He ran an impatient hand over his forehead.

Still, an interested gleam came into his eyes, she noted—the kind of gleam she was more than well acquainted with.

"Morrison called me late last night, when the world was a hell of a lot rosier, and said he wanted to give you a try. Something about a chocolate angel." He pressed his fingertips to his temples, willing his headache to either go away or kill him. "Is that his nickname for you?"

His eyes were slits now, but they watched her. "No, that's my—" What did she call Keith? Landlord? Boyfriend? Neither defined their relationship. She settled on "friend," for whatever else happened, he would always be that, she assured herself. "My friend's creation. He makes chocolate."

He smirked. "We all have our callings. Me—" he tapped his thin chest "—I make successes. I've a string of box-office hits, and I'm not easily moved by pouts, promises or swaying hips."

"How about talent?" she countered, rising.

"Spunk again," he muttered. But this time he seemed to be smiling, or grimacing; she wasn't sure which. "Okay, McKay, show me your stuff. Dance for me." He dropped into the vacated chair.

She stared at him. "With no music?"

"Now she's Julie Andrews, asking for the hills to be alive with the sound of music." He looked down into the orchestra pit. "Kenny, see if you can oblige Miss Andrews here."

Kenny looked a lot more genial than this nameless tyrant did, she thought. "What'll it be, Ms. McKay?"

She asked for "Too Darn Hot," from *Kiss Me Kate*. Before she was halfway through the number, the thin man on stage rose from his chair and ordered her to stop. Teddi began to steel herself off for another disappointment.

"Rehearsals start day after tomorrow at eight."

Teddi stared, dumbfounded. "You mean I've got it?"

"No, I want a cheering section for the players. Yes, you've got the part. Second from the end." He shrugged. "It's a start," he tossed off.

She grinned from ear to ear. "It sure is, Mr.—" She looked at him. He hadn't introduced himself. "What do I call you?"

"To my face people call me 'Mr. Cochoran.'"

"Cochoran? *Jody* Cochoran? *The director?*" He wasn't the choreographer after all, she thought in amazement. This was turning out to be the strangest audition she could have imagined. And just maybe the luckiest. Whatever Jody Cochoran touched turned into box-office magic.

He smiled at her display of awe. He liked being held in awe. "There *is* no other Jody Cochoran," he informed her haughtily. He allowed his headache to take a back seat to his much overworked libido. Even for what he was used to, she was put together rather spectacularly. A tender morsel with talent, he thought. This *was* going to be interesting.

Even in the back row, Keith could make out the sexual vibrations Cochoran was putting out. Jealousy reared, then subsided. He rose and left.

Blinking at the harsh reality of daylight, Keith shoved his hands into his pockets. He wished he'd never gone to Morrison. That man in there looked at Missouri as if she were something to be consumed. He didn't need to be up close to tell. He could hear it in Cochoran's voice.

She found him that way, body tensed, and thought he was being nervous for her. Teddi circled him before he knew she was there and threw her arms around him, letting out a war whoop that had been bubbling inside.

"I got it!" she cried. "Let's celebrate." She kissed him on both cheeks and then linked her arm through his. She began to pull him down the block. "Let's buy pizza and champagne and lick chocolate and—"

"You'll be too big to fit into your tap shoes," he cautioned her fondly.

"No, I won't be. In case you haven't noticed, I use up a lot of energy."

"I've noticed, I've noticed." I've noticed everything about you, he added silently. The way the sun highlights your hair in the morning. The way your tongue peeks out of the corner of your mouth when you're working. The way your smiles start in your eyes.

He felt excitement radiate from her and was jealous of the inanimate object that made her so joyous. "I sat in the back row."

She looked at him, surprised. And then she smiled. "What did you think?"

"I think the director's going to come on to you."

It wasn't what she had meant. She tossed her head. "I think you're wrong, but if he does, I can take care of myself."

He felt more helpless than he ever had in his life. Missouri, with her special brand of enthusiasm, had invaded every facet of his life, of his mind. How soon before she left, dooming him to feel empty and alone? He saw Emily's fate looming ahead of him. Keith balled his hands into fists. "So," he said tonelessly, confusing her, "this is what you want."

"You know it is." She touched his shoulder to get him to stop walking, but he kept on going, needing the steadying discipline of putting one foot in front of the other. "Keith, what's wrong?"

He wouldn't stop to look at her. He needed space to work this tight knot out of his chest. "You know, Missouri, dreams are a lot like chocolate. Left out in the light of day, they both tend to melt."

"Now that might be one of the profoundest things ever said to me, but I haven't a clue as to what the hell you're talking about." Exasperation highlighted her voice. "You were the one who arranged this audition for me!"

"Yeah, I know." There was no mistaking the self-reproach.

She had no way of understanding what was going on, so rather than try to hash it out, she felt it safest to let it lie for a while until it either took a recognizable shape or disappeared, as arguments had a habit of doing. Pressing her lips together, she walked silently next to him.

He had no right to do this, no right to rain on her parade. He found himself smiling. Ever since she had come into his life, phrases from musicals kept cropping up in his mind. Just because he was feeling insecure didn't give him the right to take it out on her. By brooding, he was pushing her away that much sooner.

He turned and took her hand. "Pizza first."

First hot, then cold, now tranquil. I'll take what I can get. "You've got a deal," she said happily.

She was gone just when he needed her. The rehearsals took her away from The Chocolate Dream Factory, as she insisted on calling the store, at the most crucial of times—just before his opening. Originally he had meant to run it alone, and alone was what he was each afternoon when he returned from the dispatch station. He had never known that solitude could be so depressing. A dozen times a day he caught himself wondering what she was doing. Was it all she had hoped? And had Cochoran made his move yet and intimidated her into submitting? Dancing meant the world to her. Maybe she was capable of bending a few rules to get what she wanted.

He tried not to think about it.

He couldn't help thinking about it.

"You've got your own career to think about," he grumbled aloud as he rescued a batch of chocolate just in time. A few more minutes and the mixture would have gone past the required temperature and been ruined. "Keep this up and you won't *have* a career, just sacks of ruined cocoa beans."

He worked feverishly to meet his deadline. DuBois was coming on Wednesday. He and Teddi saw each other only at breakfast and late in the evening.

"Doesn't the union have rules about long hours?" he asked testily as he shut down one oven. His T-shirt clung to him, glued to his skin by sweat.

She had walked into the kitchen to see what he was doing. With a tired groan, she sank into a chair and slipped her feet out of her shoes. "Oh, I get off at five."

He looked at his watch. "It's seven now." He didn't want to ask her where she had been those extra two hours the past three days. He wouldn't make her feel trapped just because he was shackled by his own feelings.

"I know." She rubbed her aching feet. "I stay behind to practice."

He carried a large pot over to the sink and set it on the counter. "Alone?"

"No, some of the others do, too." She leaned back in the chair and closed her eyes. When had she felt this exhausted? "It's a very demanding show."

And just what were some of the demands? he wondered.

She opened her eyes, sensing something was wrong. The perpetual hum of the machines went unnoticed. "He's coming tomorrow, isn't he?" she asked abruptly. "DuBois."

"You ought to know. You made the date."

He sounded distant again, and she wondered what it was this time. Was it tension about tomorrow? Or was it that unresolved thing that hung in the air between them?

"Are you ready for him?"

He didn't answer. Instead he took out a box of chocolate angels and held it out to her silently.

Teddi took one and ate it slowly, rolling it around on her tongue. "Are you ever ready! This tastes even better than the other batch." She was tempted to take another, then pulled her hand back. She knew there was still a limited supply.

"I added something," he said, putting the box down.

"Fairy dust?"

He had to grin at her quip. "Cinnamon. It's easier to get than fairy dust." Until he touched her hair, he wasn't aware that he was moving toward her. He brought it to his lips, inhaling the perfume. He'd missed the scent. Missed her. "The only fairylike creature I know is tap-dancing her feet off daily at the Rusk Theater."

Slowly Teddi rose. Then, as he watched, she began to tug his shirt out of his jeans. "What are you doing?" He helped her pull the shirt over his shoulders.

"Even fairies need loving sometimes. It's what keeps them flying."

He had told himself that he was going to leave her alone, that until everything was settled between them, he was going to keep his distance. One look at her face and he couldn't keep from kissing her. One kiss and he couldn't keep from wanting her, wanting the feel of her body, soft and giving, beneath his. He needed the fire that only she could create, the comfort that only she could supply.

"The same could be said for chocolate makers."

Teddi grinned, fire already singing in her veins. She ran the tip of her finger along his mouth. "We have so many things in common."

Keith drew her finger into his mouth, sending a jolt of anticipation through her.

That night he couldn't get enough of her. It was as if he were trying to store up a supply against the time when he'd lie awake at night, alone in his bed, sifting through his memories. Teddi noted the desperation and said nothing but did her best to quell it, did her best to love him with every fiber.

He couldn't make love with her like this and not want her in his life, she thought as the wee hours of the dawn crept in. He lay next to her, his breathing steady. She would have given anything in the world if this intimacy could be guaranteed for the rest of her life.

She loved dancing, always had, but it couldn't keep you warm at night, couldn't fill your heart, couldn't give you children.

Children, she mused, winding a chestnut curl about her finger without waking him. What would their children look like? He was so big, so powerful, and she had a quality of frailty about her. Would they resemble him or lean toward her? It was something she definitely wanted to find out someday.

Your children, Keith Calloway. I want your children. How do I make you want mine? How do I make you want me forever and always?

Maybe, she thought, closing her eyes and intending to get just a few more winks, after DuBois comes and gives him a rave review, he'll feel more settled and can get his mind off his damn chocolates and on me.

She felt him reach for her, and thoughts of a few more winks quickly disappeared.

Twelve

Teddi was torn. There was no way she could miss a rehearsal, not this early in the production. And especially not today. This morning the director specifically wanted to block the dance number at the end of the first act.

But she really wanted to stay with Keith and hold his hand.

Not that he had given any indication that he wanted her to stay and hold his hand, she thought as she walked into the dark theater. He had all but chased her out when she had hung back to help with last-minute preparations. Just his way of dealing with a roaring case of nerves, she told herself. He wasn't really rejecting her. Still, her stomach felt just the slightest bit queasy about the situation. She forced it out of her mind.

She walked down the aisle and wondered what the theater would look like ablaze with lights, ringing with music and teeming with people eager to laugh and enjoy themselves. Keith was working on his dream and she was working on hers.

Teddi climbed the stairs to the stage, alone with her thoughts. She sank into a chair and began taking off her shoes.

"They told me you got here early," Cochoran said, emerging from behind the curtains.

Teddi jumped to her feet, her shoes still dangling from her hand. "Oh, Mr. Cochoran, you startled me."

She looked like sunlight captured in a Monet painting. Every time he saw her, she moved him more and more. He wondered if she was really as virginal as she looked and decided that no one could be *that* innocent. "I do my best," he murmured. "C'mere." He inclined his head.

There was something about him that made her uneasy. Barefoot, she walked over hesitantly to where he stood. He draped an arm around her shoulders. Teddi tried not to be obvious, but she felt awfully uncomfortable.

He moved his face closer to hers. "How do you think the production is going?"

She stared at him, surprised. "You're asking my opinion?" Jody Cochoran never asked opinions; he pronounced them—loudly.

"Sure." He ran a hand along her arm. "You're a bright, intelligent, sexy young woman." She didn't care for the way he emphasized "sexy." "You can see things as clearly as anyone." He played with the sensitive inner side of her elbow. The message in his eyes was very clear.

Oh, no, not this, she thought. I *really* need this job. Cochoran lowered his head.

But I don't need this, she thought, summoning courage. "I think," she proclaimed loudly, turning her head just as his lips were about to meet hers, "that it's going rather well, all things considered." She sidestepped him neatly, leaving him staring incredulously at the back of her head. "I mean, it's only the first week, and we're all just learning where our feet go—"

He planted his hands firmly on her shoulders. "And where our mouths go."

She wasn't one to be bested by witticism. She looked up at him, the picture of innocence. "I don't have a speaking part."

His smile curved his lips but never reached his eyes. "That might be changed."

The Big Bad Wolf must have looked just like this when he was laying out his game plan for Little Red Riding Hood, she thought archly. If she were an artist, she would have painted him just that way. "Wouldn't the author be horrified?"

He waved his hand in dismissal. "The hell with the author. I'm in charge here."

She managed to shrug off his hands. Quickly she walked over to the edge of the stage to where she had left her things. "I thought Mr. Morrison was."

"It's Morrison's money. But it's my talent, my sweat, my say-so." He looked at her pointedly.

He was trying to impress her. Too bad he didn't know that she was impressed by tenderness, by little caring things, by navy eyes that looked into her soul. "My, my, all that power."

He moved toward her. "You're getting the picture." He began to put his arms around her.

Teddi walked off to the side. Why wasn't anyone coming? "I think it's time for a commercial break."

"Cute," he commented. "But don't overdo it. I'm not that patient a man."

Teddi pressed her lips together. "I'm afraid you're going to need the patience of Job."

He was about to ask her just what she meant by that, when voices coming from the back of the theater stopped him. "This isn't over yet," he promised her.

Teddi felt her stomach lurch as she gathered up her belongings.

"What's the matter?" the dance captain, Jackie, asked her as she walked up to Teddi. "You look like you've seen a ghost."

Teddi looked over her shoulder to where Cochoran was conferring with the choreographer. "I have. Mine. On the unemployment line."

Jackie frowned. "What?"

Teddi shook her head. "Never mind."

* * *

The morning was particularly grueling. Between the choreographer and the director, the dancers were constantly moving. Verve turned to exhaustion. It was close to twelve before a break was finally called.

Teddi couldn't wait to leave. The theater reeked of impending doom for her, of the possible end of a dream. She needed a breather to collect herself. As she stopped to pick up her purse, she listened to Jackie talk endlessly about her new boyfriend. The sound soothed her frayed nerves. It seemed to her that all morning long, every time Cochoran looked in her direction, he was silently telling her that it was only a matter of time before she'd see things his way.

Compounding that was the fact that her mind had been constantly drifting back to Keith. She glanced at her watch. In less than an hour, DuBois would be walking into The Chocolate Dream Factory.

Suddenly she felt a hand on her shoulder. She didn't have to look up. She knew it was Cochoran. With his free hand, he waved Jackie on her way. "She won't be coming with you."

Jackie hurried off, an envious look on her face.

"Why won't I be going with her?" Teddi asked.

Patiently, as if he were explaining things to a child, he said, "Because you're having lunch with me."

How was she going to handle this so that she didn't get fired? "No, I—"

He continued as if she hadn't spoken. "I know this terrific, intimate little place."

"Where?"

"My dressing room."

Teddi abruptly stopped walking. Her action threw him off-balance, making him appear clumsy. He scowled at her.

"No," she said.

He pulled her aside, away from the dissipating crowd. "No?" he asked, incredulous.

She could feel all her dreams melting. She remembered Keith's analogy. "No," she repeated.

Cochoran leaned against the wall, crossing his arms. It was impossible to see what he was thinking behind the solemn mask he wore. "Let me get this perfectly straight. You're turning me down?"

"Yes."

His eyes narrowed. "Knowing what I could do for you?"

"Yes." She tried not to let her voice quaver. There were other shows, right? But not a Jody Cochoran show.

"Knowing," his voice lowered, "what I could do *to* you if I so chose?"

She took a deep breath. He could see to it that she never worked in anything substantial again. Not on Broadway, at any rate. If she was going, she was going in style. She wouldn't let him intimidate her. "Yes," she said sharply.

"Why?" he wanted to know.

She didn't know why she was bothering to explain it to him, but her temper pushed her on. "Because I don't hop into bed, Mr. Cochoran, unless I'm in love with someone."

"And you're not in love with me."

She caught the first signs of humor nudging just slightly at the corners of his mouth. Fine lines spread out along his eyes.

"No," Teddi answered.

"A pity," he said. "For me." He uncoiled his body and stood before her. "Well—" there was a large sigh "—you can't blame me for trying. You are a stunning woman."

He was actually smiling. She had to be dreaming. "Am I fired?"

"I said I hated spunk. Scruples, though, are another matter entirely. Besides, you're good. Damn good." This time the hand on her neck was relaxed. There was no longer any tension between them. He had no more need to flex his sexual prowess. "I'd be an idiot to fire Mary Poppins." He cocked his head. "Is it the chocolate maker?"

"Yes."

"Lucky man." He began to walk off, then turned to look at her. "Sure I can't change your mind?"

This time she smiled. "I'm afraid not."

He shrugged carelessly. "You don't know what you're missing."

Teddi wet her lips. Might as well go for it all, she thought. "Mr. Cochoran?"

He stopped but didn't turn around. "Yes?"

"Can I have part of the afternoon off?"

He whirled, aghast. "What?"

If it hadn't been for what had just transpired between them, she would have backed off. But she was no longer afraid of Jody Cochoran, fire breather. As a matter of fact, she rather liked him in an odd sort of way. And there was no denying that the man was a genius at what he did. "It's very important."

"First she spurns me." He looked up, addressing some heavenly deity. "Now she wants the day off."

"Just a few hours, really. Three." She held up three fingers. "I thought that since we understood each other now and that the dancers weren't really on call until after four—I could be back by, say, three-thirty?"

He waved her to be silent. It was an imperial gesture. One he used frequently. "Take a long lunch, Mary Poppins. But don't forget to aim your umbrella back in this direction by four."

Teddi was gone before he completed his sentence.

Keith had been on his feet since five. Everything was as ready as it ever would be. Now it was all in the hands of fate and DuBois's sweet tooth. Morrison's sweet tooth had already netted him a lucrative arrangement; his accountant had been by on Monday, just as Morrison had promised. Pleased with the way Keith's books testified to his frugal management of money, the accountant recommended Keith as a sound investment. And so Dame Fortune had turned her mercurial smile on him, he thought as he arranged the latest batch of angels in one of the heavenly blue boxes the supplier had delivered late yesterday afternoon. Everything, it seemed, was happening at the last minute.

He missed her, God help him. He couldn't seem to complete a thought without visualizing her face. He didn't feel whole anymore, not even while he was doing this. How far he'd come in such a little while, he thought, looking at the chocolate angels that flew along the borders of the front room. From thinking that he didn't need anyone to needing one particular person more than he needed to draw breath.

When this was over, he was going to ask her to marry him. He didn't care about coming in second, as long as he came in.

A noise at the door caught him off guard. DuBois was early, he thought.

It wasn't DuBois.

"What are you doing here?" he asked as he walked around the counter.

They changed places. "What does it look like I'm doing?" Teddi asked, ducking behind the display counter and pulling out an apron. "I'm helping."

He put his hands on hers before she could tie a knot. "What happened?"

She saw concern on his face and it tugged at her heart. "Well, just as the director came rushing out and said, 'Kid, you gotta go on and save the show,' I thought to myself, Keith needs me. Of course the big lug won't admit it, but that's part of his appeal, I guess. So I handed in my tap shoes, told the director someone else would have to save the show, and here I am." She pulled her hands away. "Now let me tie my apron."

He wasn't fooled by her banter. Something was wrong. "Okay, now take it from the top. Why are you here instead of filling Ruby Keeler's shoes?"

"Because you need me." She searched his face. "Don't you?"

Why was one word so hard to say? He forced it out. "Yes."

She fairly beamed, desire flaring. If DuBois weren't due to arrive, she would have made love with him right there, with all the chocolate angels looking on. "There, that's settled."

He grabbed her hands. This time he held them firmly. "No, it's not settled. What happened today?" His eyes narrowed. "Did he come on to you?"

"Who?" she asked, raising her eyebrows so innocently that he had to laugh. Some of the tension left his shoulders.

"Cochoran, that's who."

"Oh, him. Like gangbusters," she said nonchalantly.

It began to fall into place. "And you quit?"

"No."

He let go of her hands and shoved his own into his pockets. "I see." He looked away.

She stared at him. Annoyance began to take hold. "No, I don't think you do. Just what is it you think you see?" She came around to face him.

"Look, Missouri, you're a grown woman—"

"Which might be part of my problem," she said tersely. She had had enough of assuming males. "Go on."

Exasperated, he threw up his hands. "What you do is your own business."

"Very true. But I kind of thought that maybe, just maybe, we were getting to know each other." Fury rose within her. How *could* he think what he was thinking? "I guess I was wrong." Unlike the fire in her eyes, her voice was stone cold.

He couldn't stand the idea of another man touching her, holding her. She belonged to *him*, damn it. And he to her. "I suppose you think I shouldn't blame you."

She slammed an empty box down on the counter. Blue tissue paper floated to the floor. "Blame me for *what*?"

"For giving in to Cochoran. Look, I know you were afraid. This was your first part, and he probably threatened to have you fired if you didn't. But don't you see—"

He didn't finish his sentence as he watched the fire rise in her eyes. She came out from behind the counter and planted a hand on his chest, pushing him back until she had him against the wall. "Do you think that little of me?"

"I don't know what to think," he shouted. "Damn it, Missouri, ever since you came barreling into my life, I haven't been able to think clearly. All I can think of is you."

The fury ebbed from her. "Go on." Her voice was soft. "This is getting interesting."

He pulled her into his arms. "This isn't the way I wanted to say it, not the way I wanted any of it to happen, but by God, it's happening."

Her eyes touched his. "Is it?"

"You know it is."

She shook her head, an impish smile flittering across it. "No, tell me."

"I love you."

It was difficult not to laugh. Inside, everything felt like the Fourth of July. "Do you always growl when you say that?"

"I don't know. I've never said it before, except to one of my pets, and that was a long time ago."

The smile that curved her lips was deep and full. "If I were a pet, I'd wag my tail now."

He ran his finger lightly along her nose. "Is that your funny way of saying you care?"

"No, that's my funny way of saying that I love you, you big jerk. Kiss me quick, before DuBois shows up."

He complied. The kiss deepened, until he was on the verge of getting lost in it. "What *did* happen today?"

She wanted more and knew they had no time. "Cochoran came on to me, all right, and I told him that I wasn't that kind of woman."

He grinned, remembering that she had once said that to him. "And?"

"And he accepted it. He even told me to take a long lunch. Seems he admires scruples. Without knowing it, I played it exactly right."

"You do have that gift," he said, kissing the tip of her nose, then each eye and then her mouth again. Her wonderful, sweet mouth.

The soft cough became louder before they even heard it. DuBois stood in the doorway, an amused smile on his face. "Am I interrupting anything?"

Teddi felt around the bed, her eyes still closed. The spot next to her was warm, but empty. She sat up, disoriented.

"Keith?" she called uncertainly.

It was Monday, her day off. The lights of Broadway were dark, and she had the entire day free. She had decided to spend it in bed—with Keith.

"Hi."

She stared at him. Keith was fully dressed as he walked into the bedroom. She knew it must be after ten, but she had expected him to stay in bed with her. Where had he been?

Under his arm was a copy of *Variety*. "Thought you might want to see the latest issue." He dropped it on the bed. "By the way, Mr. Abramowitz at the newsstand says to tell you congratulations."

"For what?" she asked, amused. "For landing in a hit play or for finally marrying a 'fella'?"

He laughed and sat down next to her. He propped himself up on the pillows. "Both. Read," he instructed, pointing to the newspaper.

Puzzled, she opened the folded paper. There, on the front page, was the typical catchy headline. Except that this time, it was about her. "Dancing Sweetie

Marries Her Chocolate Prince.'' Teddi scanned the short article below. It hailed both her promising talent and Keith's thriving business, which was growing faster than they had anticipated.

She laughed, then let the paper fall. She curled up against Keith. "Isn't life wonderful? Six months ago I was looking through this, searching for work. Now I'm *in* it?"

"Here." He tucked a folded piece of paper into her hand.

"What is this?" She opened it, then looked up at him quizzically. "These are the ingredients in your chocolate, aren't they?"

"Yes. I told you I'd let you know when the time was right, Mrs. Calloway. It's a wedding present."

She tossed the paper over her shoulder. "I don't want to make chocolate. I want to eat it—later." She raised up on her knees. The sheet fell away. "Much, much later. Right now I want to get on with my honeymoon."

His eyes swept over her. He'd never get enough of her. The thought made him smile. Forever carried a lot of promise now. "Your wish is my command."

"I like the sound of that," she murmured, falling back on the bed as he kissed her.

 **Silhouette Desire**

COMING NEXT MONTH

FIT FOR A KING—Diana Palmer
Elissa Dean was exactly who King Roper needed to protect him from
his sister-in-law's advances. The act seemed foolproof... until Elissa's
very presence set King's heart on fire.

DEAR READER—Jennifer Greene
Leslie Stuart needed to teach Sam Pierce, the country's leading
mathematician, to overcome his dyslexia. But could he teach her
to trust in his love?

LOVE IN THE AIR—Nan Ryan
More than the airwaves crackled whenever Sullivan and Kay signed
on at station Q102. But after having left once before, Kay had to
convince Sullivan that her heart was there to stay.

A PLACE TO BELONG—Christine Flynn
Rachel Summers and Eric Johnston needed each other. As a sports
therapist, she had six weeks to bring this pro hockey player back into
tip-top shape—just long enough to fall in love.

STILL WATERS—Leslie Davis Guccione
Another bride for a Branigan brother! You met Drew in
BITTERSWEET HARVEST (Desire #311)—now Ryan Branigan
and his childhood sweetheart reclaim their chance for love.

LADY ICE—Joan Hohl
Cool businesswoman Patricia Lycaster promised herself she'd be
Peter Vanzant's wife in name only. But the more she resisted, the
more determined he was to fan the desire that blazed between them.

AVAILABLE THIS MONTH:

BRIGHT RIVER
Doreen Owens Malek

BETTING MAN
Robin Elliott

COME FLY WITH ME
Sherryl Woods

CHOCOLATE DREAMS
Marie Nicole

GREAT EXPECTATIONS
Amanda Lee

SPELLBOUND
Joyce Thies

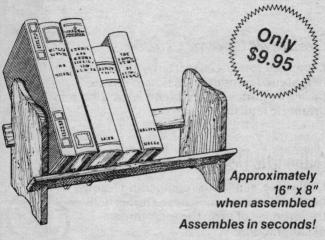

FOUR UNIQUE SERIES
FOR EVERY WOMAN YOU ARE..

Silhouette Romance

Heartwarming romances that will make you
laugh and cry as they bring you all the wonder
and magic of falling in love.

6 titles
per month

Silhouette Special Edition

Expanded romances written with emotion and
heightened romantic tension to ensure
powerful stories. A rare blend of passion and
dramatic realism.

6 titles
per month

Silhouette Desire

Believable, sensuous, compelling—and
above all, romantic—these stories deliver
the promise of love, the guarantee
of satisfaction.

6 titles
per month

Silhouette Intimate Moments

Love stories that entice; longer, more
sensuous romances filled with adventure,
suspense, glamour and melodrama.

4 titles
per month

Silhouette Romances
not available in retail outlets in Canada

SIL-GEN-1A